To my very own *Maman chérie*, who thankfully isn't at all like Sesame's.

Text copyright © 2013 Clémentine Beauvais
Illustrations copyright © 2013 Sarah Horne
First Published in Great Britain in 2013 by Hodder Children's Books. The
rights of Clémentine Beauvais and Sarah Horne to be identified as the Author
and Illustrator respectively of the Work have been asserted by them in
accordance with the Copyright, Designs and Patents Act 1988.

First published in the United States of America by Holiday House in 2014.
All Rights Reserved
HOLIDAY HOUSE is registered in the U.S. Patent and Trademark Office.
Printed and Bound in April 2015 at Maple Press, York, PA, USA.
www.holidayhouse.com
3 5 7 9 10 8 6 4 2

Library of Congress Cataloging-in-Publication Data
Beauvais, Clémentine.
Sleuth on skates / by Clémentine Beauvais ; illustrated by Sarah Horne.—First
American edition.
pages cm.— (A Sesame Seade mystery ; #1)
"First Published in Great Britain in 2013 by Hodder Children's Books."
Summary: Precocious eleven-year-old self-made-supersleuth Sophie "Sesame"
Seade investigates the disappearance of Jenna Jenkins, a student
at Cambridge University, where Sophie's father is chaplain and
her mother is Head of Christ's College.
ISBN 978-0-8234-3197-7 (hardcover)
[1. Missing persons—Fiction. 2. Family life—England—Cambridge—Fiction.
3. University of Cambridge. 4. Cambridge (England)—Fiction. 5. England—
Fiction. 6. Mystery and detective stories.]
I. Horne, Sarah, 1979– illustrator. II. Title.
PZ7.B380587Sle 2014
[Fic]—dc23
2014010154

ISBN: 978-0-8234-3453-4 (paperback)

by
Clémentine Beauvais

illustrated by
Sarah Horne

Holiday House / New York

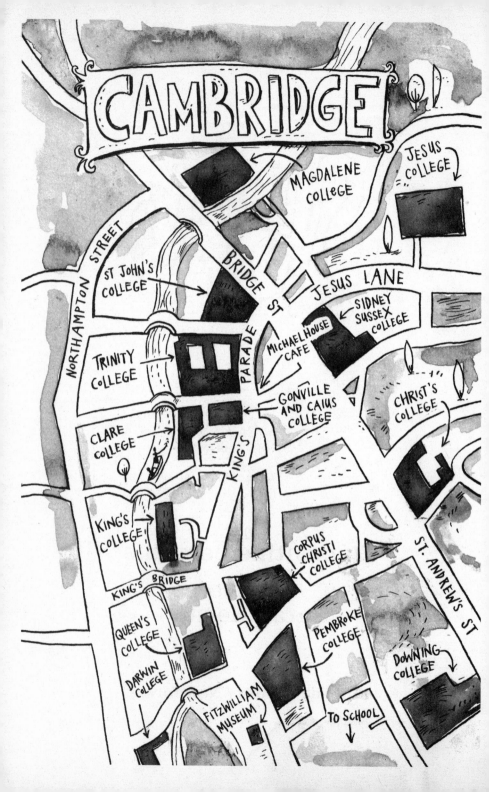

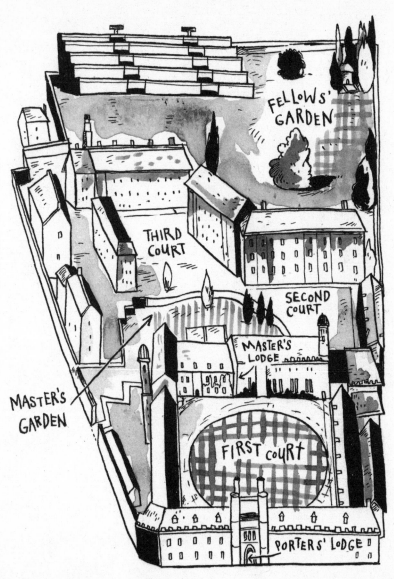

FELLOWS' GARDEN

THIRD COURT

SECOND COURT

MASTER'S LODGE

MASTER'S GARDEN

FIRST COURT

PORTERS' LODGE

CHRIST'S COLLEGE

I

You're not born a supersleuth on skates; you become one.

And believe me (me's Sesame Seade, as it says on the cover), there are more requirements than you'd think.

What you need is, primo, a pair of roller skates (purple) and secundo, this simple little philosophy of life:

If there are as many connections in your brain as there are stars in the universe, why ask for superpowers? If your feet can run and skate and if your hands can climb and swim, why want to fly?

Oh, yes, you also need a mysterious mission. And let me tell you, there aren't as many of those as there are roller skates and philosophies of life. Especially not in Cambridge, where I live. It's just a small city with a university in it, and probably the most boringly peaceful place in England, though I haven't been absolutely everywhere.

But one superior Sunday, after eleven years, five months and seventeen days of waiting, a mysterious mission found me—and at last I became Cambridge's number one self-made supersleuth on skates.

It all started very much like a normal Sunday afternoon. A normal Sunday afternoon is when my parents have all the time in the world to

ask each other bizarre questions about me. "I don't know," said Professor Seade (my mother), "whether our daughter's particularly bad manners come from a naturally evil personality or from some neglect on our behalf."

"Children are not naturally evil, darling,' said Reverend Seade (my father), 'so I'm afraid we must have done something wrong."

They both looked up at me. Up, because I was up a tree.

"What are you doing, Sophie?"

My parents, I'm sorry to say, live under the illusion that their daughter is called Sophie Margaret Catriona Seade, which makes no sense. Call me Sesame.

"I'm playing with Peter Mortimer and my binoculars."

"Don't look into students rooms: it's rude."

"Mother, I never look into students' rooms. It's either boring or disgusting."

Living around students isn't easy, but I have to endure it because my house is in a college, and colleges are where the university stores its students. They sleep there, eat there, work there, and produce a lot of noises and smells in the process.

I live in a college for parent-related reasons: my mum is the Head of Christ's College, Cambridge University, Cambridge, United Kingdom, Earth. That makes her the local queen. That makes me the local princess, which means I can cross that off my to-do list: good to get it out of the way. As for Dad, being married to Mum could make him the local prince consort, but he prefers to be the college Chaplain.

"Tree to Earth, Tree to Earth! Warning! Peter Mortimer is getting ready to jump down!"

They didn't listen to me.

"Earth, do you copy? Peter Mortimer is in jumping down mode, something serious!"

Still didn't listen.

"That's Peter Mortimer, Charlie-Alpha-Tango! Crash expected in three-two-one ..."

They should have listened, because Peter Mortimer landed on Dad's head, and apparently it hurt.

"That cat!" said Dad. "I'll have his dirty claws removed!"

"I'll have you know that God created every single one of his dirty claws!" I protested.

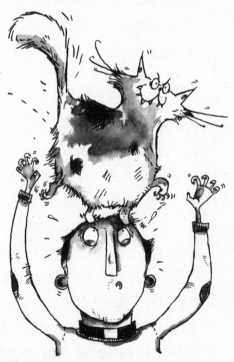

"The problem with Sophie is that she's a manipulative little Gorgias," sighed Mum.

My parents' favorite sentences follow this simple recipe:

1. *Sigh*

2. *"The problem with Sophie is that she's a"*

3. *negative word*

4. *"little"*

5. *obscure name.*

Once in a delicious blue moon, I get:

1. *Smile*

2. *"The good thing about Sophie is that she's a"*

3. *positive word*

4. *"little"*

5. *obscure name.*

"Get out of the way, Chubby! Go back into the house!" said Dad.

My parents, I'm sorry to say, live under the illusion that Peter Mortimer is called Chubby. I don't think it's fair to name someone after a weight problem. Understandably, Peter Mortimer resents Dad and Mum. He brings them dead things to express his violent feelings towards them. Like now.

"Oh, not again! Chubby, can't you leave the mice alone?"

"Well, Mother, how ironic."

Mum slaughters twenty mice a day. She's a Professor of Therapeutics, which means she makes lab mice sick, tries to cure them, and fails most of the time.

"How does she know what ironic means?" asked Dad.

"God knows. She must have heard it from one of the students."

Not one to blow my own trumpet, but I seem to have a taste for sophisticated terminology, which means difficult words.

"I have a theory to explain Peter Mortimer's passion for hunting," I said.

"Let's hear it then," Mum muttered.

"It's all based on a big misunderstanding. When Dad says 'Let us pray' six times a day,

Peter Mortimer thinks he means 'Let us prey'."

I had to explain, because they couldn't see the difference like you can.

Dad sighed. "The problem with Sophie is that she's a blasphemous little Thomas Aikenhead."

I wouldn't want you to think that my parents don't really care about me. I could see through my binoculars that Mum was reading an article in *The Sunday Times* called "The Joys and Sorrows of Having an Only Child," and circling things with a pencil.

"Tree to Earth! Tree to Earth! Earth, do you copy?"

"For goodness' sake, what is it now? Can we never have a peaceful Sunday?"

"Porter approaching fast! Collision with garden expected in three-two-one—"

Knock-knock!

Mum got up, folded her newspaper, and crossed the garden to open the tiny green door, behind which stood Tod the Porter. Porters are the sleepless sentinels and guardian angels of the college. They know absolutely everything

about the place
and its students,
and believe me,
there are things
you really don't want
to know about the latter.

"Hello, Tod," said Mum. "Please come in. Everything all right?"

"I'm afraid not," replied Tod, walking into our garden. "You know the student I told you about this morning?"

"Goodness me, she's still missing?"

"We thought she might have gone home unexpectedly, but we've just spoken to her parents—she's not there."

"Who's missing?" I asked.

"Oh, hi, Sesame. I hadn't seen you up there."

"Hi, Tod! Who's missing?" I asked louder, as they'd all suddenly gone a bit hard of hearing. Through my binoculars, I could see Tod looking at Mum, who looked at Dad, who looked at me.

"Don't scream like that," said Mum. "One of our students has disappeared. Tod, I think it's time to call the police. I'm sure it's nothing, but we can't take any risks. I'll be through in a minute."

"Who is it? Maybe I can spot her with my binoculars. Maybe she's stuck on a roof like the last one."

(Edmund Sutton, last year. He stayed stranded on a roof for a whole Friday in the manner of Robinson Crusoe.)

"She's called Jenna Jenkins," said Tod.

I looked everywhere on the roofs for someone who looked like a Jenna Jenkins, but in vain.

"Roof hypothesis tested and eliminated," I declared.

No reply. Dad had gone to wash the blood off his scalp. Mum and Tod had gone to the Porters' Lodge, at the college's entrance, which is the best place for the Porters to check with their laser-beam eyes that only tourists and students walk in and out of college (as opposed to chainsaw-wielding serial killers). Peter Mortimer was inside, thankfully, because the only living being left in the garden was a pregnant-looking duck who was eyeing the stream at the bottom of the garden. I climbed down the tree and walked into the house.

"There's a pregnant duck outside."

"Ducks don't get pregnant, darling; they lay eggs."

"She shouldn't stay here. She's going to get ripped to ribbons by Peter Mortimer."

"Don't roller-skate in the house."

"Too late, they're on now. Daddy, did you know Jenna Jenkins?"

"Yes, vaguely. Goodness, be careful, you're going to break something."

"Did she have any known enemies?"

"No, and please don't try and play Sherlock Holmes. The police will do what they need to do. Watch out, that's fragile! Have you done your homework?"

"This is my homework."

"What, bulldozing our living-room carpet?"

"No, learning things about the world. That's what school is for, the Head said. Bye, Reverend!"

"Where are you going?"

"Roller derby."

First Court in Christ's College has got one big circular lawn with a stone path around, which makes it an awesome roller derby track. And it echoes like inside a cave. It's my favorite Sunday activity (I don't tell Dad that).

"Hi, Sesame! Enjoying your weekend?"

Fiona Lumley is one of my best friends among the students. I try not to get too attached to them because, like rabbits, they only last three or four years and then they're gone. But Fiona studies medicine so she'll be around a bit longer, therefore I allow myself to be a little bit attached. Being friends with students is like adopting big siblings, I guess, but without being able to sneak into their rooms to read their private diaries. Well, unless you know where to get the keys from.

I braked as if I was about to fall off the white cliffs of Dover, Fiona covered her ears, and when the screeching noise had receded I replied:

"Not really, I don't like Sundays. They have this habit of leading to Mondays. But exciting things can happen: have you heard about the mysterious disappearance of Jenna Jenkins?"

Fiona frowned, and combed her hair with her fingers.

"Yes, I have. I don't know her very well, but I think it's much more worrying than they're making it sound. She's been missing for two days. Everyone assumed she'd just gone home. But she hasn't."

"Unless she did go home, and her parents sold her as a slave."

"Somehow, I doubt it. And it's all the more mysterious as she was about to play the leading role in this year's Ballet Society show—*Swan Lake*. She'd been going on and on about it for weeks."

"I think," I said (joking), "a rival probably chopped her up like an aubergine for a ratatouille and drowned the pieces in the river Cam."

"I think," said Fiona (not joking), "we may have to consider that something sinister has happened to her."

"Did she have any known enemies?"

"Plenty," replied Fiona. "She's not only a ballet dancer. She's been Editor-in-Chief of *UniGossip* magazine for two terms, and she hasn't made many friends in the process."

II

"Maman chérie, light of my life, can I go out for a walk?"

"No."

"Papa chéri, fire of my loins, can I go out for a walk?"

"For Heaven's sake, Sophie, where did you get that terrifying expression from? And no, you may not go out for a walk. It's nine o'clock. You should be in bed."

Sophying me around is the best way of getting me to disobey. I was outside in no time at all. My bedroom window is just above a little terrace where the big tree leans on its elbow. I slid down the trunk and landed on a bunch of tulips. The pregnant duck was still there.

"Are you nuts? You shouldn't stay here. Peter Mortimer's going to bazooka you to the grave and munch on each little bone of each of your little ducklings."

The duck shrugged and jumped into the stream, which is not wise. The fish in there are enormous; I hate them all, with their moustaches. Even Peter Mortimer can't catch them, and they laugh at him.

"Now, to business."

The Porters' Lodge was quiet when I reached it on tiptoe. Don, the Porter on duty, was drinking tea and looking at his computer screen. In the stealthy manner of the leopard, I crept up to the desk, and then did a forward roll, because that's the done thing for a supersleuth.

It was so astonishingly perfect that a "Wow!" escaped my mouth. Thankfully, at the very same time the phone rang and Don picked it up.

This was the opportunity of a lifetime. I broke into another three forward rolls. They weren't as good as the first one and I sort of ended up head first in a cardboard box, but I finally reached the pigeonholes with only a few paper cuts on my forehead.

Now if you think that pigeonholes are actually full of happy pigeons, you are sadly deluded: this word is a wildly deceptive lie. Pigeonholes are students' mailboxes. They are barely big enough to fit two letters, let alone a pigeon (I've tried, and been punished).

I skimmed through the names on the stickers.

Jameson, K.

Jameson, M.

Jared, M.

Jeng, W.

Jenkins, J.

Jenna Jenkins's pigeonhole.

With nothing in it.

Of course, the police must have cleared it all. That was not an encouraging start to my sleuthing career.

I stood there scratching my head and looking at the disappointing nothingness, until something appetizingly colorful caught the corner of my eye and I got distracted. You would have got distracted too, for that something was a medium-sized box of Quality Street sweets, standing there unopened on the floor!

A little bit of yellow paper was taped to it, which said:

For Jenna J.

I lifted it, and the following note appeared in full pencilled glory:

Where ARE you?? I waited at Auntie's Tea Shop for ages yesterday and you never showed up. You're not answering your phone or replying to emails! What's going on?

Hope you're OK! Let me know! I still don't know what you want me to do for UG.

Jeremy X

I congratulated myself for being so much better than the police at spotting essential pieces of evidence and grabbed the box of Quality Street. Then I had to flatten myself like plaice against the wall when Don hung up the phone and stood up to take his empty tea cup back to the kitchenette.

That's when I noticed the copy of *UniGossip* on the Porters' desk. As soon as Don had whistled his way to the next room I stretched out my free hand, bagged the magazine, and legged it into the dark and stormy night.

That had been a fantastically successful first mission, I thought, hopping back into

the garden. To celebrate I sat down in a bush and ate just a few sweets until there was hardly anything left in the box apart from a nice little pile of multicolored wrappers. The pregnant duck looked like she was craving the strawberry-flavored one, so I let her nibble on it and she quacked enthusiastically.

Then I realized I'd eaten up the evidence and felt a little bit guilty. But at least I hadn't eaten up the yellow message.

Jeremy.

There was a Jeremy in this story. I didn't exactly know when he'd delivered that box of sweets to Jenna, but at that time she'd already disappeared, and he was already worried.

I still don't know what you want me to do for UG.

I picked up the copy of *UniGossip*. Blood-red headlines and blurry photographs stared out at me:

LAW PROFESSOR CAUGHT SHOPLIFTING AT ASDA!

University Team Rower Secret Father of Twins!

WHO'S THAT WITH YOU, VICE-CHANCELLOR? CERTAINLY NOT YOUR WIFE!

It didn't sound like the kind of magazine I'd be reading in my spare time, as it didn't come with a free gadget and didn't have any comics in it, but I shuffled through it and found the Credits page. Jenna Jenkins's name was mentioned on top, as Editor-in-Chief, and right underneath it, another name:

Jeremy Hopkins—Chief Investigator.

The pregnant duck looked at me with one of those puzzled looks that ducks have.

So I whispered to her: "What sizzling-hot scandal could Jenna Jenkins have discovered that made her mysteriously disappear before she could ask her Chief Investigator to investigate the case?"

Cambridge is the windiest place in the universe. As I fell asleep I could hear the gale howling and screaming and whistling as it rushed through the stone flames of the towers.

But Sesame Seade isn't scared of the dark or the wind.

III

"The problem with Sophie is that she's a self-obsessed little Narcissus."

"Mummy, my tie has absolutely got to be tied in the right way, or else I might catch Mr. Halitosis's virus when he tells me off."

"Mr. What?"

"Mr. Halitosis. You know, my teacher?"

"Mr. Barnes, you mean?"

"Mother, you are five centuries late. That used to be his name, as in, on the very first day of school, before we noticed what was wrong with him. We called him Mr. Deathbreath for a while, but then Gemma's mum told her bad breath was actually a medical condition called halitosis. So to be more respectful and accurate, we now call him Mr. Halitosis."

"You've been in front of that mirror for eighteen minutes."

"And it's worked wonders. The tie is perfectly tied. You may call for my carriage."

"No need, the carriage is already calling for you."

Indeed, I could hear yonder our little blue Twingo hooting and honking like we'd won the World Cup.

"Oh, Dad's in command of the Smurfmobile today?" I asked. "Why not you?"

"Because—hurry up, for goodness' sake— because in exactly one minute and forty-eight seconds, some very important people will be knocking on the door to discuss very important matters with me."

"About Jenna Jenkins?"

Mum sighed one of her legendary sighs. "No, not about Jenna Jenkins. We still have no idea what happened to her."

"Who is it then?"

"Jesus Christ, Sophie Margaret Catriona!"

"Is that his full name?"

"You are such a pest. You're not even going to be interested. They're from Cooperture Ltd, the largest marketing agency in the country. Happy?"

"No. Atrociously disappointed."

"Go!"

I went.

"Have a nice day at school!"

I did.

My best friends at school are called Gemma Sarland and Toby Appleyard. I selected them on the basis of their abilities.

Gemma always wears pearl earrings and lives in a huge house in Waterbeach, which is

a deceitful place parading as a tropical heaven when it is, in fact, just a normal Cambridgeshire village.

Toby lives very close to school. In fact, he lives at school. His mum is Mrs. Appleyard the school caretaker and his dad is Mr. Appleyard the school cook. Mr. Appleyard's food is odious. Toby's used to it, but Gemma and I aren't yet, and we have to be nice and swallow everything and pretend that we don't detest it. That is the main inconvenience of being friends with Toby.

Our school is called Goodall and isn't all bad.

"I have astonishing news," I said to Gemma and Toby immediately. "A student at Christ's has simply ceased to exist."

"Dead?"

"God knows. Gone, for sure."

"Did she say where she was going?"

"No, or it wouldn't be a true disappearance."

"Who is it?"

Frustratingly, Mr. Halitosis decided it was time to start telling us about geometry, forcing us to continue conversing in the form of scribbled notes.

"Pythagoras's theorem . . ." said Mr. Halitosis.

She's a ballet dancer, I scribbled in turquoise. **Like a tutu dancer.**

Epic fail! wrote Toby in highlighter.

". . . states that the squared length of the hypotenuse . . ."

She's also the Editor-in-Chief of *UniGossip*, which is a magazine with lots of scandalous things in it, I pencilled on.

Why would anyone want to find her? Good riddance, retorted Toby's black ink pen.

STOP IT, it's serious, answered Gemma

sparkily (I don't know where she finds her pens). **She could have got killed! I know tons of ballet dancers and they're the meanest people on this side of the Equator!**

"...is equal to the sum of the squared lengths of the other two sides ..."

How do you know tons of ballet dancers? interrogated my red marker.

"...in a right-angled triangle ..."

It was starting to look pretty, all these colors. Gemma's revelation was pale green:
Because I'm playing cello in *Swan Lake* this year, remember?

"Sophie Seade, what is Pythagoras's theorem?"
Mr. Halitosis crossed the classroom and Gemma, Toby and I immediately switched to no-breathing-allowed mode.

"Yes, you can blush, my dear child," he said (I wasn't blushing, just running out of air). "You haven't been listening to a word I said."

"On the contrary, Mr Barnes," I replied, using my air in a controlled fashion developed over months of practice. "Pythagoras's theorem is all about how the squared length of the hypotenuse is equal to the added squared lengths of the other two sides. Of a right-angled triangle, of course."

Mr. Halitosis stayed still for a moment, and then he said, "Oh good," and went back to his desk. We breathed in some non-polluted air, and our lungs said thank you.

And that is an example of what you can do when the number of connections in your brain is at least equal to the number of stars in the universe.

At break, Gemma expanded on her stupendous revelation.

"My dad met someone who was looking for cello players for the University Ballet show, so he said why not Gemma? And I said no thanks, but it was too late, and now I have to rehearse every two days on top of all my homework and I'm the youngest there and the producer's horrible. It's dire."

"So you must know Jenna Jenkins!" I exclaimed. "She dances in that ballet!"

"I don't know them all by name. What part does she play?"

'The lead. I don't know the story, so I'm assuming it's either the Swan or the Lake."

"The lead is called Odette, you ignoramus," scoffed Gemma. "OK, I know who she is. But if she's been wiped off the surface of the Earth, who's going to play her part? Someone must be, because I have rehearsal tonight at six."

Notwithstanding my profound hatred of tutus, I realized it was part of my sleuthing duties to endure it just this once.

"Gemz, I will come with you to rehearsal this evening."

"Oh, yes, please do. It's so boring being around these old students. You're used to it, at least."

"That's unfair," protested Toby. "I was just going to ask you both to come over to my house to watch a film after school! My mum bought me new DVDs over the weekend. I got *Wall-E*, and *Anastasia*, and *Spiderman* . . ."

"Sorry, Toby. We can't be distracted from our important mission. But I'm putting you in charge of extracting top-secret information from the depths of the Internet. Find out all you can on Jenna Jenkins. It's crucially vital."

He agreed. "OK, then. Oh, good news! Dad told me this morning that we're having roasted chicories with lard for lunch!"

Gemma and I urghed in unison.

After school and before Gemma's rehearsal we had two hours to do exactly what we wanted.

"Well, not really exactly what we want," retorted Gemma, unfolding her scooter. "We can't go and raid the old sweet shop, for one, since we don't have balaclavas."

That was indeed a shame. "However," I remarked, "we can pretend that we've just raided it, and that every tourist holding a camera is a police officer with a flamethrower."

Gemma thought this was the best idea since the other one I'd had two hours earlier about adopting a grasshopper. So I slammed the clasps of my roller skates into place and we left school, rattling along the pavement at high

speed in the white afternoon sun and dodging
the deadly camera flashes of the tourists (which
in Cambridge is no small feat). Ducking and
bending, we managed to whoosh past all the
buildings up to King's College, but suddenly—

"No! One of them got me!" screamed Gemma.
"I'm completely on fire!"

He'd almost got me too, but I'd leapt over
the low brick wall and landed flat on the lawn,
which earned me some furious glares from the
Porter at King's gate, since walking on the grass
is the deadliest sin.

"Sesame, are you mental?" said Gemma. "I
don't want to spend the rest of my life visiting
you in prison."

"To be fair, it was that or being turned into

hot embers by a flamethrower."

"Well, I've been turned into hot embers, so let's call it a day and go to your place to dig out some chocolate from your dad's secret cupboard."

I wiped my green hands on my shirt, jumped over the wall again and grabbed on to Gemma's burning clothes to pick up a bit of speed. But as we turned the corner of the street, my right eye caught the name of a place and it rang a bell. I braked and pondered.

"What's wrong?" asked Gemma, braking too. "Are you on fire after all?"

"No. I'm having an 'ah-ha!' moment. Look: Auntie's Tea Shop!"

She looked bewildered, so I had to explain

that Jeremy Hopkins's message to Jenna Jenkins mentioned that very teashop, and that it was a unique opportunity to investigate.

"Maybe this place is Jeremy Hopkins's favorite feeding ground," I asserted. "Let's go in and see if he's there. He might give us important information about Jenna Jenkins."

"Who cares? They're just students."

I forgave Gemma for that remark. It's true that students are generally not very interesting. But this time, there was kidnapping and possibly murder in the air.

"I'll only be a minute. Keep an eye on my roller skates."

Merrily, I kicked them off and walked into Auntie's Tea Shop. Unfortunately, no one in there looked like they could possibly be Jeremy Hopkins. Even more unfortunately, someone in there looked like she could very possibly be my own mother.

"Sophie Margaret Catriona Seade! In the name of all that is holy, what are you doing alone in here?"

Mum, wearing her best apricot dress, was surrounded by smug-looking men in suits. In the soft jazzy music of the place, they were nibbling on slices of a blueberry cheesecake which I warmly recommend.

"My dear Maman," I said, curtseying to the floor, "good afternoon to you and to all your friends. I saw you through the window and could not resist the urge to pay you my respects."

"I see," said Mum in a voice that meant "Liar." "Gentlemen, this is my daughter, Sophie."

"Pleased to meet you, I'm Sesame," I said. And then I waited to be introduced, so Mum could not but introduce me.

"Sophie, these are Mr. Franklin and Mr. Mukherjee from Cooperture, and this is Ian Philips, an eminent professor of Ancient Greek from the Department of Classics."

I shook hands with the whole bunch.

"And what are you doing this afternoon, Sophie?" asked Professor Philips in a smooth, deep voice. "Your mother seems surprised to see you here."

"I'm just skating back from school with my friend Gemma."

"Is this the route you usually take?"

"Not at all," said Mum. "The problem with Sophie is that she's a deceitful little Judas. We never have any idea what she's up to. Why are you only wearing socks?"

"I left my wheels outside under Gemma's watchful eye."

While Mum was frowning rudely at my socks and the hole in one of them, I glanced at the table. Among the cups of tea and slices of cake there were pieces of paper with complex-looking words. I eyed a few figures with several zeros.

Professor Philips coughed and Mum said, "Sophie, go home, please. We're actually in an important meeting."

"Please can I please go and watch Gemma's rehearsal of *Swan Lake* tonight at six please?"

Mum's eyebrows said "No" but in the atmosphere of general amusement she eventually muttered, "All right then. Where is it?"

"West Road Concert Hall!"

"How will you get there?"

"I'll go with Gemma really fast and we won't talk to any strangers!"

"How will you get back?"

"I'll ask Dad to pick me up!"

Mum rolled her eyes, nodded and let me go, for which I was grateful.

"How was it?" asked Gemma as I squeezed my feet into my roller skates for the third time that day.

"Catastrophic. I bumped into my mum."

Gemma shuddered from head to toe. She's scared of my mum. I used to be scared of my mum too, until I started scaring her back.

"Well," she said, readjusting her tie, "I had a more useful time waiting here outside. You'll never guess what I found on the pavement."

"How many guesses do I get?"

"Three."

"A small piglet."

"No."

"A smoky meteorite."

"No."

"The Crown Jewels."

"Almost. Look."

I looked, and it was a crumpled-up five-pound note. "That's super lucky of you!" I exclaimed. "What are you going to do with it? Of course you can do whatever you want and don't need to share with me whatever you buy with it."

"Of course I'll share," she said (thankfully). "If you hadn't asked me to wait here I wouldn't have been bored enough to look at the pavement. Come on, let's get a box of tangy tangerine strings at the old sweet shop."

So we picked up speed again and whooshed past a cluster of tourists and overtook a

pushchair-pushing person and almost got run over by a gangly student on a bike and slalomed around a man in a wheelchair with a robotic voice.

And then the worst happened.

'Sophie Margaret Catriona Seade!'

Seriously! Parents!

I braked wearily and turned around to face Dad.

"What on Earth are you doing in the street on your own?"

"Good afternoon, dearest Papa. How coincidentally beautiful to find you here! It must be the Almighty guiding my steps to you. And I am not alone! Gemma's here too."

He twirled around but didn't

see Gemma, who was hiding behind a burly student because she's also scared of Dad.

"Right there," I said, and she had to show herself, looking meek. "You see, Daddy, Gemma won the pavement lottery and we were about to splash out on tangy tangerine strings."

"Certainly not. Does Mum know you're here?"

"Your mum, or my mum?"

"Who do you think?"

"Here *here*, or here in *Cambridge*?"

"Where do you think? Listen, Sophie, I don't have time for this. But since I strongly suspect that Mum—your mother, my wife, Professor Seade—has absolutely no clue that you and Gemma are roaming the city center like street urchins . . ."

"We're not that prickly!"

". . . you shall both come with me and stay with me during my meeting with Reverend Tan.'

"But Daddy . . ."

"Hush!" he hushed in a way that made us both follow him in silence. He pushed a glass door to a church converted into a café and sat us down at a table.

No tangy tangerine strings would tingle our tongues today. We shot surly glares at Dad, who asked, "All right. What do you want?"

"An electric guitar."

"What do you want to drink?"

"Whisky."

"Goodness!" he eructed, and he went up to the counter. "Two glasses of freshly squeezed orange juice and a cappuccino, please. Oh, hello, Frederick."

Frederick, alias Reverend Tan, had just walked in. Like Dad, he was wearing a dog collar. Unlike Dad, he still had all his hair and no wrinkles. Unlike Dad, he didn't look angry. In fact, he looked positively terrified.

"My daughter Sophie and her friend Gemma," groaned Dad as he and Reverend Tan sat down at a nearby table. "Girls, this is Reverend Tan, the Chaplain of Trinity College."

I stopped slurping and said, "How do you do? I'm Sesame."

Gemma said, "How delightful to meet you.

I'm Gemma."

Dad said, "Do your homework."

We got our books and notebooks out of our bags and Gemma started trying to figure out what Pythagoras was about and how to use his theorem to answer the questions properly.

"Darling daddy, do you have a pen I can borrow?"

"You don't have any pens? What's that pencil-case for?"

"Well, see, it does contain pens, but also a grasshopper, so if I open it now it'll go hopping everywhere."

Dad blew out a lot of air, fished out an expensive fountain pen from a pocket of his shirt and said, "Now you'd better be silent."

Since I had such a good pen, I couldn't waste the ink on geometry, so I started writing a poem of despair and anguish at the absence of Jeremy Hopkins and the possible imprisonment of Jenna Jenkins in a dark rat-infested cave. It was stupendously goosebump-inducing.

Meanwhile, Dad and Reverend Tan were talking, and part of my brain was listening to them while the other part of it was being poetic. That's another thing you can do when the number of connections in your brain is more or less equal to the number of stars in the universe.

"What is it, Frederick?" murmured Dad. "Your message got me worried. Is it that bad?"

"It is a serious matter, and I don't know enough about it, nor feel that I can do anything about it. It's a question of . . ."

He turned his head towards Gemma and me, and I went into removed-from-the-world-of-the-living mode. His voice was so low I had to intensely strain my stirrup, which is the smallest bone in the body (located in the ear), in order to hear it.

"I have evidence . . ." he whispered, "Well, . . . at least, a student has told me that she has witnessed serious illegal activity at her department."

"Which student?" whispered Dad.

"I cannot say, David."

"Frederick, in such a situation . . ."

"I don't mean that I feel I shouldn't. I mean

I don't know who she is."

He glanced at me again (seriously, do I look more suspicious than Gemma?) so I pretended to stare at an ugly abstract painting on the wall that looked like someone had thrown up Smarties on a canvas.

"You see," he said, "I've set up an online anonymous chatroom called Ask-a-Vicar. Anyone in the university can talk to me one-

on-one, on any matter, every evening, over the Internet. Yesterday night, a person using the screen name 'Tsarina' started talking to me. She said she was a female student—she wouldn't say any more. And then went on to tell me that she knew someone was doing something illegal at her department. Something that could have an impact on the whole university. But before she could tell me what it was—literally just as she was about to say it—the college's Internet suddenly went down, and I never managed to speak to her again."

I felt like I'd stumbled from a fairly fun dream into a much spookier one. Jenna Jenkins, I thought. It must be Jenna Jenkins. But yesterday, she'd already gone missing . . .

"Jenna Jenkins," murmured Dad as if he'd read my thoughts. "Have you heard . . . ?"

"It was not Jenna," said Reverend Tan, shaking his head. "I know her—she's interviewed me in the past for her magazine. And I'd heard about her disappearance, so I thought of her immediately. But it couldn't have been her."

"How can you be so sure?"

"Jenna's dyslexic, she's told me a few times how difficult it is when you want to be a journalist. But that girl—the one I talked to on the Internet—her spelling was impeccable."

Dad looked dubious for a moment, as if it was easy-peasy for a dyslexic to fake impeccable spelling. Then he said, "Well, Frederick, I think you should pass this conversation to the police. They'll be able to trace it back to the computer and—"

Frederick gave a sour laugh. "I would be thrilled to pass everything to the police. Unfortunately, my computer was stolen from my room this very morning."

IV

Thankfully, Dad let Gemma and me go to West Road Concert Hall on our own. I think this was mainly because he thinks highly of Gemma.

"Right, Sophie, I'll pick you up at 7:30."

"Sir, yes, Sir!"

"You are actually going to this rehearsal, right? You're not going to run away?"

"Sir, no, Sir!"

He gave the clouds a God-give-me-strength sort of look, my forehead a kiss, and started walking back. Gemma unfolded her scooter in a few clicks, and we rushed forth into the city.

"What was that about?" she asked in a wobbly voice as she scooted over an irregularly-cobbled patch of pavement. "Illegal activity? What kind?"

"You were listening?"

"I was all ears!"

"Me too! That's probably why we're friends. What do you think? He didn't say much, apart from the screen name. Tsarina. Do you have any idea what it could mean?"

"Well, apart from a Russian princess, no."

"A Russian princess?"

"Yes, Sesame, a tsarina is a Russian princess. That's what they're called."

"How do you know that?"

She replied, "I know everything about the royalty of every country." This only surprised me a little, as she does wear pearl earrings.

"Right. So a Russian princess witnessed illegal activity at her department."

"No. There aren't any Russian princesses any more. Russia killed all its royal family ages ago. A tragedy."

"Weird. I wonder if this not-Russian-princess found out anything to do with Jenna Jenkins's mysterious disappearance."

"Can't see any reason why they're related," shrugged Gemma.

"I can't either, but my sleuthing radar is picking up suspicious signals."

"What's a sleuthing radar?"

"A special sixth sense for signs of scam and scandal. If you need to ask, it means you haven't got it," I declared, and squinted to try to make the signal clearer (which didn't work).

Gemma sneered, "Thank goodness for that. Apparently, having it makes you look like a right loony."

So I switched the radar off and we reached West Road Concert Hall, from which

unpleasant musical noises were escaping. I took off my roller skates, put on my shoes and followed Gemma into the temple of tutus. Her folded-up scooter clanked melodiously against her shoulders.

Two musicians, a boy and a girl, holding immense instrument boxes, were chatting in a corner. Another three were at the bar.

"Right," I whispered to Gemma. "This is your moment. Go and interrogate people about Jenna Jenkins."

"Seriously, Sesame! You can't ask me that. Do it yourself."

"No, I can't, people always think there's something fishy about me, whereas they'd beg to store their butter in your mouth if fridges didn't exist. Come on, do it—I'll pretend I'm your foreign penfriend."

Gemma started shaking a little bit, but I poked her in the ribs and she leapt forwards and landed right next to the two instrument-holding students.

"Hey," she mumbled, "how're things?"

"Who are you?" replied the boy in a voice that made it sound like meeting us was only slightly better than kissing a dung beetle.

"Gemma. I'm in the orchestra," she said. "I play the cello. This is my penfriend Sesame . . . er, I mean . . . Sashimi."

"Sashimi?"

"Yes. She's Japanese."

The two students stared at me in mild disbelief, for which I don't blame them. There's a reason Gemma isn't Cambridge's number one self-made-supersleuth.

"Anyway," said Gemma, "me and her, I mean she and I, were wondering if perhaps you know where Jenna Jenkins is."

"Why?" the boy asked.

"Because," replied Gemma in a strained voice, "because . . . well, Sashimi wants to . . . er . . . invite her to Japan . . . to dance . . . at the Emperor's annual Yule ball."

I rolled my eyes so forcefully that I managed to get a glimpse of my own brain.

"Listen, I think I know what you're playing at,

kids," said the girl. "You've heard that Jenna's disappeared, and you thought you'd have a little detective game. Am I right?"

Gemma said, "Yes."

I said, "Ie!" which means "no" in Japanese, but no one understood.

"Well, I'm sure you've got better things to be doing with your time," said the girl. "Jenna simply decided to leave Cambridge, everyone here is sure of that. Too much pressure, too much competition. Nothing mysterious at all."

"Who's replacing her?" asked Gemma.

"Her understudy, Stacy Vance. That's what understudies are for."

The boy checked his watch. "OK, Shauna, we'd better go. And you too, Gemma, if that's your real name. It's time."

Forgetting that I was Japanese, I erupted, "Wait a minute—Stacy Vance? What's she like? Does she have a murderous sort of personality?"

The girl burst out laughing and turned back. 'You've got the wrong suspect there, love. Stacy and Jenna are best friends. Stacy's absolutely distraught that Jen's disappeared. She's been looking for her all weekend."

And they vanished into the wings.

I paced to and fro for a while, wondering if Stacy Vance could have chopped Jenna Jenkins into tiny cubes and drowned them in the river Cam just to get to play her part, but eventually I made my way to the huge concert hall. From the orchestra pit rose the screeches and whines of the violins and cellos. I hate string instruments. The sound gets inside your head like it's sawing through your brains. I don't tell Gemma that. She was inside the pit, scraping her bow against the strings like all the others. She winked at me, and I blinked back for want of winking ability.

"What are you doing here, young lady?"

I turned around. It was a student about as tall as me and as big as me, but with a bow tie, and who looked vaguely familiar.

"I'm friends with Gemma Sarland."

"Who?"

"The one there with the pearl earrings and shameful Mr. Men knickers."

"What? Where?"

"There. She's wearing a skirt, you'll have to take my word for it."

"And who are you?"

"My name is Sesame. How about you, pray?"

"Edwin. I'm the producer." He looked at me mysteriously as if to unlock some invisible trapdoor on my forehead. "Go and sit down. It's going to start."

He followed his own order by sitting down and getting his laptop out. I sat down a few rows up, wincing at the cacophony coming from the orchestra pit. When it failed to stop, I realized it was actually the beginning of the ballet. A dozen tutu-waggling ballerinas came onstage in a pointe walk that was so noisy it sounded like someone was enthusiastically hammering a bunch of nails into a tambourine. After a great number of what I'm assuming were grands jetés and pas de chats, someone tiptoed onstage who could only be Stacy Vance. She was so swan-like I wouldn't have been surprised to see her fly.

After ten minutes of this frilly rigmarole, I started to tire. There's only so much tulle tulip-shaped tutu twirling one can take. So I left my seat and skipped out of the concert hall and into the wings.

In the wings, there were more wings: a huge stack of feathery wings. As I wondered what on Earth these wings could be doing there, I heard the hammering noise again and quickly jumped behind an old piano, peering around the side of it. The army of ballerinas had emerged from the dark curtains that led on to the stage, and each stopped to pick up one pair of wings, which they clipped to their backs and ironed out with their fingers like a strange flock of coquettish cockatoos.

"What do you think?" whispered one of them to another one of them.

"About what?"

"Stacy, of course!"

"She's good enough."

The first girl nodded, and looked around. The others were busy ruffling each other's feathers. "What the hell is up with Jen? Everyone's so cool about it. Seems to me like no one actually cares where she's gone."

"She's so unstable, Kim. You've only been here this term, you don't know. Jen's just the sort of person who'd run away from a stressful situation."

"Really? She seemed strong enough."

"It's all fake. She's a bundle of nerves. If you ask me, it was too much pressure. This part, plus her exams, plus *UniGossip* . . . No wonder she couldn't cope."

The first girl looked unconvinced, but suddenly the music changed and they had to leave again, fluttering to the stage like skinny angels. I relaxed a little, and sat down against the back of the piano.

And then realized I wasn't the only one there.

"Nice to meet you," said the other one, "I'm Jeremy Hopkins."

I shook his hand. "How do you do? I'm Sesame

Seade. Do you come here often?"

"It's my first time, but I won't come back, the service is terrible."

"I'm glad I've finally bumped into you behind this piano. I had a few questions to ask you. What were you and Jenna Jenkins going to talk about during your meeting at Auntie's Tea Shop that she never went to?"

"Wait a minute," he said. "What's all this about? How do you know about Jenna Jenkins?"

"It's not going to work if we keep asking each other questions. The basic rule of a dialogue is to alternate questions and answers."

"Right-o, smartypants. I'll answer your question. Jen and I were supposed to meet up at Auntie's on Friday afternoon. She vanished that very morning. We were going to be talking about *UniGossip*."

"She was going to ask you to investigate something. What was it?"

"I have no idea. We can't discuss things like that by email or text—only face to face. She'd only told me that it was something big. Very big."

"You don't know what it was about?"

He rubbed his fingers together. "Money. What else? Anyway, what brings you here?"

"I also happen to be investigating the mysterious disappearance of Jenna Jenkins."

"Splendid. Let's compare notes."

He actually got his notebook out. I felt very unprofessional. "It's all in my head," I said, and that was true—it's the best notebook I have. I lose all the other ones. "So, what have you found out?"

"Not much more than what I've already told you. I think the last person she talked to on Friday was Edwin—he told the police he'd phoned her to discuss something costume-related. Now, what have you got?"

I was a bit embarrassed there because my findings were more or less equivalent to zero. Of course I'd had time to think of many colorful ways in which Jenna Jenkins might have been minced up, and the Tsarina mystery was interfering with them on my sleuthing radar, but none of this would convince an experienced Chief Investigator like Jeremy Hopkins. So I said, "Well, to be fair," and stopped.

"Right," he laughed. 'OK, listen. I think no one's worried enough about what's happened to Jenna. Everyone seems to think she left of her own accord. But that's not the kind of thing she'd do. I know her well, it takes guts to run *UniGossip*. I think she's been forced to leave. If not worse."

"Dead or alive, we'll find her!" I promised fervently.

"Do you even know what she looks like?"

I had to admit I didn't, and he got a photo out of his pocket. The lighting was bad but you could see a thin bird-like girl, wearing bright clothes, surrounded by a great quantity of opened and unopened presents, including a blue teddy bear, a bottle of the same perfume as my mum, and a pair of ballet shoes.

"It was taken at her birthday party, in October."

The unpleasant hammering noise started again, and the fluttering squad flooded in. In a few seconds, they unclipped their wings and flung them to the floor, ruffling a pile of brochures. One of them took off like a dove and landed next to me.

"What's that?" I said.

"Just the program," replied Jeremy Hopkins. "They have to reprint them all, because Jen's not Odette any more."

It was a slick-looking thing, with a big green

and white C in a circle to symbolize Cambridge, I guessed, and the words *Swan Lake*, in elaborate spirally writing.

I shuffled through it. Half a page was devoted to telling the reader everything about Jenna Jenkins's life so far. Nothing I didn't know before. Next was a pompous picture of the producer from a professional photo shoot, and in enormous letters:

Edwin Franklin, Third-Year Student in Classics, Trinity College.

The blurb babbled on about his achievements. I skimmed through the rest. Gemma's name was mentioned among a hundred others in the orchestra.

"Anyway," said Jeremy, "I came here to listen to what people were saying in the wings, but I only overheard people congratulating each other. I don't think Jenna's disappearance is linked to the ballet. I think it's more sinister than that."

Onstage, the music died out.

"Let's get out of here before the tutu battalion comes back," said Jeremy.

We jumped to our feet and left the wings, blinking in the neon light of the entrance hall. When my eyes finally managed to focus, they focused on a stunned-looking vicar.

"Oh no," I sighed.

"Sophie! What on Earth were you doing in there?"

"Just having a look around, Daddy. I've concluded that ballets are more interesting backstage."

"Who is this young man?" said Dad in a voice that meant, "Who is this scoundrel?"

"That's Jeremy Hopkins," I said obligingly.

"And what is Jeremy Hopkins doing here with you?"

My words were so good that Jeremy Hopkins nicked them: "Just having a look around. I've concluded that ballets are more interesting backstage."

Dad shot him a hundred terrifying glares. "Why are you hanging out with my daughter?"

"I didn't know she was your daughter," replied Jeremy.

The answer didn't seem to satisfy the holy man, whose nostrils frilled up in the manner of the huffy buffalo. "Right," he said. "We're going home."

"Daddy Daddy Daddy, I have an urgent question."

"What is it?"

"Is the pregnant duck still in the garden? I'm worried, you see, because if Peter Mortimer sees her it's going to be World War III."

Jeremy Hopkins chuckled, Dad obliterated him with another discharge of angry glares, then he ruffled my hair and said, 'Yes, love, it's still there, but I thought of you and looked up a few things on the Internet about ducks.

Apparently, it's trying to find a place to settle down and lay eggs. Tomorrow I'll move it to Emmanuel College. They have a pond there, and no cats."

"Oh, Daddy! I'm so proud of you! I'm sure God is really proud of you too. I bet he didn't know you had potential as a bird-relocalizer. Maybe that's your new calling!"

"Yes, well. Let's go."

"Bye, Jeremy!"

"Bye, Sesame!"

And we walked home in the purple night.

V

Tuesday morning introduced itself rudely by shooting a painful ray of sun right into my opening eye. The garden was drowned in sunlight, the towers and gargoyles shone white. Peter Mortimer, flattened out in the manner of a bearskin, was on the terrace outside my window, purring like a diesel engine.

"Today, I'll find Jenna Jenkins," I promised the world.

But before that I had to get dressed for school, and as I was putting on one sock, Peter Mortimer leapt on the other one and kidnapped it just like that.

"Peter Mortimer! Give that back, you vicious velociraptor!"

But the sock-hijacker dived out of the room and tumbled awkwardly down the stairs. A second later, he'd slipped into Mum's study to hide the indispensible piece of clothing under her desk.

"You are such an obnoxious example of felineness! I will have you hanged high and short!"

Knowing himself to be under the protection of God and the East Anglian Cat Lovers' Society, Peter Mortimer didn't budge, and I had to crawl under the furniture to dislodge the hissing monster from his lair. When I finally managed to push him out of the study, I was bleeding from all sides like a hot-water bottle in a hedgehog's bed.

And then, since I was in Mum's study, which doesn't happen that often, I thought I might as well have a little look around.

"Best Mummy in the world, queen of all mummies, endlessly beautiful model of mummyhood?"

"What have you done again?"

"Well, you see, admirable Maman, it all happened very accidentally. A treacherously slippery floor sent me flying into your study, and then my tie tied itself around the handle of the middle drawer of your desk, and it slid open, and suddenly a massive gust of wind hooked out a single piece of paper . . . "

"For goodness' sake, Sophie! You've been looking through my desk?"

"I can't have done, Mother, it's made of solid wood."

"You know what they say about curiosity."

"Yes, that's why I made sure Peter Mortimer was out of the room. Anyway," I stated before she could retort, "this single small rectangular piece of paper somehow landed in my hand, and try as I may, I couldn't help but notice . . . "

"Cut it, Sophie. You found the cheque. What of it?"

"Six hundred thousand pounds, Mum! Six hundred thousand pounds! How many bags of sea-salted caramel fudge is that? I can't even represent it in my head! If I close my eyes and scrunch up my face like this—see how scrunched up it gets —like this—even if I do that, I can't imagine it in my brain . . ."

"Good, because it's not the kind of money I

want my eleven-year-old to be able to imagine. Why do you only have one sock?"

"Who in the universe could possibly have given you all that money?"

Mum rolled her eyes and dropped a few extra sugar lumps in her tea. "It's not mine, you featherbrain. It's for Christ's. For the College. To buy new books for the library and help a few students pay for their university fees. It's a donation from Cooperture."

"A donation? Why?"

"I'll have you know, my dear, that it is extremely frequent for colleges to receive donations from sponsors. When you barged into Auntie's Tea Shop yesterday, you interrupted a very important meeting I was having with the President and the Vice-President of Cooperture, and with Professor Philips who put us all in touch. Luckily, they mustn't have been too appalled by your shockingly disgusting socks, because they made very generous donations to ten different colleges, including Christ's. There might be more in the future. It is a very large sum of money, but there's no reason to be so shocked."

"But why give all this money away? Do they have too much?"

Mum rearranged her eyebrows in a way that made it clear she was explaining difficult things to a small child, took my hand, and said slowly, "No, darling. It's in return for exposure. That's what companies do. Cooperture gave us all that money in exchange for the installation of a piece of software on the college's Internet system. Now every time students open the Internet in college, they see the word 'Cooperture' written at the top of the page. And that is all."

"So they might buy things from them?"

"No, Cooperture is a marketing agency, they don't make things. They just work for companies that do. They tell these companies how to get people to buy more of their products, and they help them sell them by making adverts. Anyway, it's too complicated for you to understand."

"What's the point of advertising themselves then?"

"The point is . . . Well, the point is that students might then want to apply for a job at Cooperture."

"But then they'll have to pay them again for the salaries!"

"Yes, but over several years the students might make them money."

I shook my head. "I don't understand. It doesn't make sense! Giving all that money just because in ten years' time a student from Christ's might earn it back for them?"

Mum let go of my hand and laughed, looking at the ceiling. "Oh, Sophie! Why do you even care? Don't worry about Cooperture, they have enough calculators and people who know how to use them to make absolutely sure that their investment will be worth it."

"But Mum, don't you find it weird . . ."

"Why do you only have one sock? We're leaving in five minutes!"

"No news from the police about Jenna Jenkins?"

"No! Will you ever start minding your own business? Get ready, or else!"

So I got ready, because else isn't pleasant when Mum's involved.

I met up with Toby and Gemma in front of the chalky white columns of the Fitzwilliam Museum.

Mr. Halitosis decided three weeks ago that we were to spend a whole morning there in retribution for Stephanie Paulson telling him that art was only good for dusty old people like him. It wasn't very fair of Stephie: it isn't even dust, it's dandruff. And he's certainly not as old as his suits.

"Sorry I couldn't say bye yesterday," I said to Gemma. "My dad forcefully removed me from the place."

"No problem, we had to stay there for ages anyway, to meet Edwin's dad."

"Edwin's dad?"

"Yeah, he's given Edwin money to help pay for the show, apparently, so I guess he wanted to check that we hadn't all bought ourselves diamond tiaras and supercars. Did you find anything interesting?"

"Lots! But nothing links together. Or to Jenna Jenkins. It's like life is sending me on ten paths at the same time!"

"It's a problem we all have to face," whispered Mr. Halitosis, and his whisper poisoned an unlucky fly who breathed its last buzz and fell to the floor.

"Come on, children, hush, we're going into the museum. Solal, do not stick your bogey to that sculpture. Emerald, why are you crying? What do you mean, she stole your hair? It's still there, my dear. Oh, I see, apart from that patch here—Dani, that wasn't nice of you. Look, children! This is an authentic Greek statue. Why are you chuckling, Benjamin? Yes, it is very small, but at the time it was quite rightly perceived to be a sign of manliness."

As the others gathered around the sugary-looking marble statues, Gemma, Toby and I were still conspiring on the side.

"I found something on the Internet," said Toby. "An interview with Jenna Jenkins for *The Cambridge Student*, in which she talks about her little brother who's disabled. She said she wants to be successful to be able to pay for better care for him."

"Interesting," I said, "but not linked to her mysterious disappearance."

"Psychologically notable," concluded Gemma. "But we have to find out what she'd discovered. It's the only way to understand what happened next."

"Are you enjoying Greek art, children?" said a soft voice above our

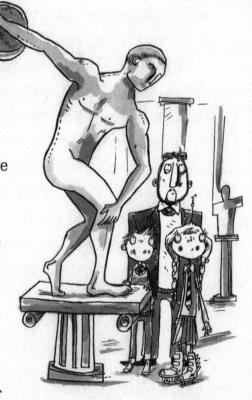

heads. "Why, I think we've met before, Miss Seade."

Black moustache and rimless glasses. My brain generally sends my parents' pals' faces to the recycling-bin of my memory pretty fast, but since I'd met that one only the day before in Auntie's tea room, I remembered he was Professor Philips.

"*Kalimera*, respectable Greek Professor," I said affably (that is to say, trying to sound like Gemma). "What are you up to on this sunny day? These are my friends Toby and Gemma, by the way."

Unfortunately, Toby was just demonstrating a karate move which he was planning to use on Jenna Jenkins's kidnapper when we'd finally cornered the bandit. Professor Philips twirled around and met Toby's foot before being properly introduced to Toby himself. The encounter took place right in the middle of his belly.

"Humph!" humphed Professor Philips.

"Uh-oh, I'm going to be in trouble," prophesized Toby.

And then we realized it was snowing envelopes in the manner of the legendary scene at the beginning of *Harry Potter*, except that the envelopes were emanating not from a fireplace but from Professor Philips's leather briefcase.

"I'm so sorry," said Toby, "my foot decided you were a kidnapper."

The professor spat a few words which I assume were Greek and sounded threatening. Then he dusted off his shirt, on which the pattern of Toby's sole was now neatly printed. Gathering his letters on the floor, he groaned, "A kidnapper indeed! I was simply on my way to the post office."

"And you decided to do a detour via the museum?" said Gemma in a dubious voice.

"No, I work here. My office is downstairs," replied Professor Philips icily.

As he was attempting to justify his suspicious conduct, I bent my neck to a painful 90° angle and read the address on the top envelope:

Prof Seade
Masters Lodge
Christs College
Cambrige CB2 3BU

"Oh! That's my mother!" I exclaimed.

"It is indeed," commented Professor Philips. "Now, let me go through, you dangerous gang of terrorists."

"Wait,' I said, "give it to me and I'll deliver it myself! I'll put it in a little bag and then, tonight, I'll put on an orange visibility jacket and get my bike out and say 'Postman! Postman!' and drop the letter into the letter box with lots of junk mail, and then run away from the dog! (Though we don't actually have one, as it would infuriate Peter Mortimer.)"

"Thank you very much, but no," said Professor Philips rudely. "This is a matter between your mother and me."

"I really think you should consider Sesame's offer, it'd save you a stamp," said Toby.

"Will you leave me alone?" moaned the erudite man. And he was gone.

"Who was that?" questioned Gemma. 'He didn't look like the kind of person you'd usually hang out with."

"He's not," I said, "he's just pals with my mum."

"Oh, I see. Why is he all weird about it? Do you think it's a love letter he's sending to her?"

"Are you insane? What kind of deranged lunatic would be in love with my mum? No, it must be about all that money she's getting from some marketing company. He's been helping her rake it in like Scrooge McDuck."

"He looks like a right bore," said Toby. "Did you see how mental he went when my foot connected with his stomach? Oh, no, we've lost the rest of the class! Run, or we'll get pulped to death by Halitosis.'

As Toby and Gemma sped up to the next room, an alien body crunched under my shoe. I looked down with half-open eyes, dreading to see the corpse of a very small mouse, which

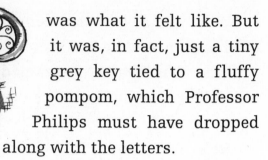

was what it felt like. But it was, in fact, just a tiny grey key tied to a fluffy pompom, which Professor Philips must have dropped along with the letters.

A part of me said "Finders keepers." Another part said "Render unto Caesar the things which are Caesar's," which is one of those things that Jesus said in funny English. Normally I would have followed Jesus's advice, since my dad works for his dad, but this time I had reason to believe that Caesar was actually not involved in this affair at all. So I pocketed the key and joined Toby and Gemma and the rest of the class and Mr. Halitosis, who was showing profound ecstasy in the presence of a decorated pot.

The rest of the visit went smoothly, until Mr. Halitosis handed out the packed lunches which Mr. Appleyard had prepared for us. Mr. Appleyard believes that children must eat more milk-based products per day than a cow can make in a year. Consequently, our sandwiches were composed of butter, cream cheese, and a slice of Red Leicester. Following this was yoghurt, and two Babybels per person. For drinks, we got Chocomilk.

Gemma was the first person to be sick, and chose to be so at the top of the marble staircase. Ben, who always copies everyone, was sick six seconds later. Soon the staircase looked like the Niagara Falls, Mr. Halitosis began to tear off what little hair was left on his head, and the museum staff discovered that there was only one mop in the whole building.

"Don't worry," I said to Mr. Halitosis, "my stomach is as stable as the Leaning Tower of Pisa. I'll just run next door to the Anchor and ask for extra mops."

I don't know if he heard me, but I ran to the pub before he could say no. I know the Anchor very well—my cool godfather Liam takes me there when he comes to Cambridge. The boss is called Sam, and his son, Peter, manages the punt-renting company right next to it.

"Peter!" I screamed, tumbling into the pub.

"You must run at once to the Fitzwilliam Museum with at least twenty mops! You will find the entrance flooded by white-looking sick, my teacher moping on the side, and museum staff overwhelmed by the event."

This didn't seem to spur Peter into action. "The thing is, Sesame, well, I'd love to help, but I'm waiting for a delivery of mini-canoes. It could be here any minute . . ."

"I'll wait here," I said, "and take the delivery. I'll stay outside the burrow like a watchful meerkat, and tell the delivery people where to store the ships."

Peter had no choice but to go, and he'd only been gone a minute when a big white van backed into the parking space and an athletic-looking man—not unlike the Greek statue we saw before the great sick epidemic—jumped out.

"Heya," he said, "you're the manager's daughter?"

"Sadly not," I said. "My parents' jobs are completely not as cool. I'm just helping him out while he's on a mission."

"Where do I put this?" asked the moving-Greek-statue man, lifting half a dozen canary-yellow canoes from inside the van.

I took him to the hangar behind the pub and he dropped the boats and six small paddles in there, alongside a bunch of inflatable jackets.

"They look like valiant vessels," I said. "Are they difficult to steer?"

The Greek laughed. "Not sure you can even

talk about steering, love. You just sit in there and splash around with the paddle and it moves. My two-year-old could do it."

"I'm not sure Health and Safety would like that," I remarked.

"Right. Well," said the irresponsible father, "I'll just go. Tell Peter we'll settle up later."

I wanted to leave him a tip, but I only had a tube of Mentos, so I just waved goodbye. Peter came back two minutes later, reeking of sick, with his nostrils squeezed together.

"Dammit, Sesame, what I wouldn't do for you."

"You've been heroic. Your canoes are inside the hangar."

I shook his hand, which was sticky, and walked back to the Fitz, where Mr. Halitosis was in fits. Parents were waiting outside to take their pale and shaky children home, and though most of them complained loudly at being disturbed at work they all seemed pretty pleased about it. Toby, of course, wasn't sick—he's had to get through eleven years of Mr. Appleyard's food, after all.

"Success!" I rejoiced aloud to him. "I haven't been sick, which means that for once in a lifetime, my parents won't be around!"

"Wrong," replied Toby, "your dad's over there."

Shock horror, he was tragically right. It was Reverend Seade, no doubt about it, chatting with someone in a suit on the other side of the entrance hall.

"Father," I declared, planting myself in front of him, "leave at once. I am in perfect health and do not require parental assistance."

"What?" said Dad.

"I am so not sick that I even took a delivery of six canoes and an equal number of paddles and life jackets."

"Are you crazy? Where will we put them?"

"No, I mean at the pub."

"Heavens! What were you doing in a pub?"

"The museum staircase was in urgent need of spring-cleaning, so I went to ask for extra mops."

"I have no idea what you're talking about," stammered Dad. "I'm not here for you. The problem with Sophie," he sighed to his mate, "is that she's a self-centred little Omphalos." And turning back to me, 'Sophie, this is Professor Philips, a computer scientist at Trinity College. We're here to have lunch in the museum café."

"Professor Philips?" I repeated. "But Professor Philips left the museum hours ago. And he certainly didn't look like that!"

"There is no need to point an accusing finger at Professor *Archie* Philips for not looking like his brother, Professor *Ian* Philips," said Dad.

"Not a problem," said Professor Ian Philips's brother Professor Archie Philips, shaking my hand. "Nice to meet you, young lady. Your father and I have known each other since we were young men."

"Nice to meet you, old gentleman," I replied obligingly. "My father and I have known each other since I was born."

"Sophie, can you please leave us?" implored Dad, looking a little weary.

I was happy to oblige.

There were eight survivors from the intoxication and we all congratulated each other on our stainless steel stomachs before heading back to school, dragging a comatose Mr. Halitosis by the hand. As we reached the school gate, I said to him, "Isn't it amazing, Mr. Barnes? All these torrents of milk-scented vomit and we didn't even feel slightly queasy! Even with those little bits of undigested bread floating around in it! I call it a victory."

But then I realized Mr. Halitosis wasn't listening any more: he was too busy being copiously sick into a bush, and the radioactive whiffs were spreading at lightspeed with every retch.

Since it would have been unfair to make us do maths and history while the others were at home being granted all their dearest wishes by their parents, the Head asked Mrs. Appleyard, who has a passion for animals, to come and tell us exciting facts about them. We saw the cruel python swallowing an entire bulldog, and the fearless cheetah running after an antelope, and the incredible gliding squirrel falling from branch to branch with just a square of skin stretched between its arms and legs!

And then we were allowed to go and do cartwheels on the school field, and inside the classrooms the other kids were pretty jealous of our super stomachs.

"Look!" said Toby, dropping a paper boat in the river Cam which runs along the bottom of the school grounds. "It'll end up in Grantchester!"

"No it won't. The river flows the wrong way."

Rivers are very contrary. We waved goodbye to the scintillating ship on its long journey, and hoped it would discover unexplored lands in the manner of Christopher Columbus.

And then it was time to go home, and I realized I hadn't done anything today which could possibly enable me to find Jenna Jenkins.

VI

This is the moment when the proud supersleuth, faced with defeat, collapses into a podgy armchair and sips on a drink with many ice cubes.

"In the name of all that is holy, Sophie! What's in that glass?"

"Apple juice on the rocks, Maman. It adds to the atmosphere. Look, if I take it in my hands and swirl it around like this, it tinkles. Exactly like a detective film."

"Your father's just told me he found you and Gemma on the street on your own yesterday afternoon. Didn't I tell you to go straight home?"

"Well, you did say 'go home,' but there was

no 'straight' between 'go' and 'home'."

Mum rolled her eyes and sighed. "I didn't know teenage crises started so early."

"With her, it started at two years old," Dad commented.

They both recoiled in horror at what I assumed were stressful memories.

"DAD!"

"Goodness me! What is it now, you shrieking gibbon?"

"I completely forgot to ask you about the duck!"

"Was there any need for the Australians to hear that? The duck is safe. It's at Emmanuel College. It's made lots of new friends. Happy?"

One of us wasn't happy, and that was Peter

Mortimer. As he walked into the room I saw he was in a foul mood. His prey had all been removed. This morning the sock, now the duck. Tough luck. I fished the mysterious key out of my pocket.

"Lookity look, kitty darling baby," I said soothingly, dangling the pompom under Peter Mortimer's nose. "That's almost as good as a pregnant duck!"

He hit it with his paw, glared at me and strutted out of the room, making sure I could see his bum.

I looked at the ruffled pompom. Under the fluff, a thin strip of white fabric had appeared, with numbers on it. **3901**. As I pondered on the meaning of these numbers, Mum shot a suspicious glance at me and said, "What's that?"

"Nothing."

"It's not nothing, it's a key."

"And, more interestingly, a pompom."

"Where did you find it?"

"On the floor."

"Where on the floor?"

"Can't remember."

Mum looked at the ceiling as if to beg it to collapse on my skull. "You are impossible!" she exploded. "If by tomorrow you haven't taken that key back to where it belongs, you will be in a lot of trouble! Is that clear?"

"Yes, Mummy."

"Are you sorry?"

"Yes, Mummy."

"What do they do to thieves?"

"You don't fool me! I'm too young to go to prison. I'm protected like the Queen's swans."

"Go to your bedroom and think about your actions!" screamed Dad and Mum in perfect unison, which confirmed what I've always suspected, which is that they got married to form some kind of double act.

I went to my bedroom pretty quickly and thought about my actions. And as I thought about them I realized how atrociously naughty I'd been, and cried bitter tears of remorse unto my pillow, whimpering: "Ah! Wouldst that I had never picked up this key! Wouldst that I had taken it to the Lost Property office! My parents are right—I should be thrown into gaol and given only breadcrumbs to peck on!"

(Gaol is pronounced jail.)

Oh! What could I possibly do to set things right? What had Mum said? If I hadn't taken that key back to where it belonged by tomorrow, I would be in serious trouble. Now what did she mean by *by tomorrow*? It was already seven o'clock. Maybe she meant tomorrow evening. But surely it was wrong to keep a lost object for that long. Maybe she meant tomorrow lunchtime. But Professor Philips might need his key in the morning! Which meant Mum must have wanted me to return it by 12:01 tonight, which was effectively tomorrow.

That was the only possible interpretation.

She wanted me to leave the house after dinner and take the key back to where it belonged before the clock struck midnight.

Between you and me, it surprised me a little, as I wouldn't have expected Mum to allow me to go to the Fitzwilliam Museum on my own after dark, but then parents' moods are as changeable as the Cambridge wind.

"Are you going to bed already?"

"Yes, it's getting a bit late."

"It's only eight forty-five. Are you ill?"

"No, I'm just particularly tired. Look! AAahhhh."

"I don't think I absolutely need to witness your yawns. Good night, then."

"Good night, Mummy! Good night, Daddy! Good night, wisteria! Good night, chandelier! Good night, moon!"

"Go to bed!"

I went to my bedroom and quickly put on my supersleuth uniform, which is, for want

of sewing abilities, my school uniform and my roller skates. I threw the roller skates out of the window and slid down the tree to the garden. I escaped through the small green door and crossed Third Court, praying I wouldn't bump into any obnoxious Fellow who'd tell my parents everything about my escapade. "Fellow" is the official name for university teachers, but let me tell you, "jolly good" is never guaranteed to go with it. Like my parents, most of them seem to think I shouldn't be roaming the premises on eight wheels. Or any number of wheels, actually, as one Fellow duly informed me one day when I crashed into her office window on a unicycle.

Having successfully not bumped into any of these unfunny people, I left College through the back door, put on my roller skates, and the dangerous Cambridge night swallowed me up.

To be fair, it was actually quite well lit, and it didn't seem as dangerous as my parents had always told me. Instead of muggers and child-snatchers, I whizzed past old ladies and students carrying orange Sainsbury's bags. One of them I recognized. . . .

"Hi, Fiona!"

"Sesame! Your braking technique is terrifying. What are you up to?"

"I'm on a sleuthing mission. You mustn't tell my parents."

"It's not as if I had coffee with them every day. Nothing dangerous, I hope?"

"What do you mean by dangerous? Crocodiles, vampires, arsenic?"

"You don't have to answer," said Fiona. "Okay, I'll see you around."

"Yes! Oh, what's that T-shirt? It's well cool!" She was wearing a hoodie with a drawing of a stethoscope around the collar, and medical instruments scattered all around in pockets.

"It is, isn't it? I got it free in the post this afternoon. It's some promotional thing from a T-shirt company. Fun coincidence, since I'm studying medicine!"

She left, waving goodbye, and as I watched her go, I noticed on the back of the T-shirt a C in a circle that looked vaguely familiar.

I picked up speed again and whooshed past the market place and Great Saint Mary's church, which chimed nine o'clock. Big and low in the dark brown sky, the full moon dusted the top of King's College chapel with whitish light.

Finally I got to the Fitzwilliam Museum, its slim columns turned silver in the night.

The large iron bars were all locked, so I threw my roller skates above the stone railing and climbed over. I landed on the grass and walked to the side door.

It was locked, of course. What had I expected? I twisted my wrists, looking at the sky. I was gravely unprepared! But then I noticed the code-lock keyboard on the side of the door, and I keyed in 3901. The door clicked open and I walked in.

I don't know if you've ever walked on a museum floor with just socks on, but it's the most amazing thing ever. It's like ice-skating. I couldn't stop myself. I slid through the Greek antiquities, did a triple axel in the ceramics room, fell down and almost broke my crown next to an Egyptian stone. Then I remembered I was on a mission. What reminded me was a white door with a simple business card inside a clear rectangular plastic holder:

> Professor Ian Philips
> Ancient Greek History
> Fellow of Trinity College

"Ha!" I said. "It's the door."

So I slipped the key inside the keyhole, and turned it to the right.

Nothing happened.

I turned it to the left.

Nothing happened.

I left it in there and said: "*Alohomora*!"

Nothing happened.

I left it in there and said: "Open, sesame!"

Nothing happened.

I was a little stunned. And then something added to my stunned mood.

That something was the sound of footsteps coming down the corridor, accompanied by two voices:

"We already have results. It's working."

"Good. Money well spent."

"And well earned."

"Mainly thanks to you."

"Couldn't have done it without your art of persuasion."

Not only did the conversation make no sense, but I was trapped. Trapped in a corner where there was only one door that wouldn't open, and . . .

And a broom cupboard! Which I tried. Which was locked. Locked! Who locks a broom cupboard? No wonder there weren't any mops available earlier!

The footsteps and voices were getting closer.

"Is she OK now, by the way?"

"She's fine. We negotiated."

"How much?"

"Doesn't matter. I'm more concerned about that Tsarina person."

Tsarina. Part of my brain recorded that, whilst the other part was trying to figure out how to open the broom cupboard. That's the kind of thing you can do when the number of connections in your brain is equal to the number of stars in the universe.

Use the key, said a little brain cell.

I was inside the broom cupboard before I even realized I'd unlocked it.

Outside, the footsteps had stopped.

It was the Philips brothers, no doubt about

it. I recognized their voices—Ian's smooth and deep, Archie's higher-pitched and merry.

Fumbling noises were heard.

"Don't tell me you've lost your office key as well," said Archie.

"Ah, no, here it is. Still no idea where the other key is, though. Thank goodness I lost it after she'd gone."

"Can you imagine?" whispered Archie. "Can you imagine if she'd still been in there?"

"Yes, well, it didn't happen, did it? No need to worry about it."

Professor Philips's office door opened, and I heard the noise of a light switch being flicked on. From a vent at the top of the broom-cupboard wall, three bars of light shone through from the office.

104

That's when I realized that the broom cupboard was deeper than I'd thought. Furthermore, it had no brooms in it. Unusually for a broom cupboard, it contained an air bed (deflated), a sleeping bag (rolled up), a pile of *Tintin* books and an empty box of McVitie's biscuits.

And then my head formed a thought which had been waiting patiently in the back of my nose for a little while. That thought was that the cupboard kind of smelt like my mum had been in there.

This surprised me a little bit, as my mum isn't the kind of person who'd snuggle up into a museum cupboard to munch on hobnobs and chuckle her way through a pile of comics. So there had to be another explanation for the waft of perfume which was unmistakably the same.

And suddenly the explanation exploded out of nowhere. The birthday picture Jeremy had shown me. Jenna Jenkins surrounded with gifts. A blue teddy bear. A pair of ballerina shoes. And a bottle of perfume. The same as my mum's.

Jenna Jenkins had been here.

And Toby's foot had been right. Ian Philips was the kidnapper.

If Mum had known, I don't think she'd have sent me on this mission.

Inside the office the two Professors weren't talking much any more. All I could hear were clickety noises and electronic beeps. Of course there can be very innocent reasons for spending an evening with your brother typing away at a computer. They could have been cobbling together a nice photo album for their mummy's birthday. But I had reasons to believe that it wasn't exactly what was going on.

Not only had Professor Ian Philips kidnapped Jenna Jenkins, but Professor Archie Philips had known everything about it. Even now that they'd released her, it didn't look like they were up to any good. And they'd confirmed what my sleuthing radar had been beeping on about: that Tsarina, somehow, had something to do with

Jenna Jenkins's mysterious disappearance. But what?

After ten or fifteen minutes of this suspicious silence, I pushed the cupboard door open and made a stealthy escape, taking the key with me. I couldn't leave it there; it had my fingerprints all over it—what if the police found it and thought I was Jenna Jenkins's kidnapper?

I left the museum, climbed over the railings again, and put on my roller skates. The city was very dark and silent as I rushed past the stone buildings. I flung the key into the Cam and sneaked into college through the back door.

Peter Mortimer was waiting for me on the little terrace. As I jumped into my bedroom I heard footsteps on the stairs, and just had time to leap into bed and close my eyes before the door silently slid open, casting a long rectangle of orange light inside.

Two shadows. Mum's voice: "Yes, she's asleep."

Dad: "Hugging her roller skates."

Mum: "Don't ask."

VII

"What's all that junk?"

"Well, that's a nice way of saying good morning, Father."

"I wasn't talking about you, Sophie. I'm talking about that."

"What is it?"

"A catalogue on duck-rearing that came in the post this morning, addressed to me!"

He looked at the object as if it was a time bomb, and put it down on the table. It was called *Happy Ducks* and, appropriately, was decorated with a picture of a smiling duck. Just underneath the duck, there was the small C in a circle I'd seen on Fiona's T-shirt and somewhere else. I flicked through the magazine. It was full of very useful objects that the keen duck-breeder would need. Duck food! Egg incubators! Little coats for ducklings!

"That's amazingly cool," I said. "I think we should try it! Look, you can get a beginner duck-rearing kit from only £124.99! Can we? Can we?"

Dad just rolled his eyes and picked up the *Telegraph*.

"Good morning, Mummy, are you in a good mood?"

"Why? Do you have something to confess?"

"Yes."

"Then if I'm in a good mood it's very likely to change. What is it?"

"Well, please don't make me reveal my sources, but I have splendid evidence that Jenna Jenkins's kidnapper is none other than Professor Ian Philips, probably helped by his brother Professor Archie Philips. They locked the poor girl in a broom cupboard in the Fitzwilliam Museum."

Mum looked at Dad, who looked at Mum, and

they both produced vexingly loud laughs. Dad smiled and said, "The good thing about Sophie is that she's an imaginative little Scheherazade."

"No, seriously, parents, you have to believe me. He kidnapped Jenna and left her to rot with only a box of biscuits and a pile of comics in a cupboard. I don't know where she is now, but that's the absolute truth. And Archie Philips is involved in the Tsarina affair! And they both use the Fitz as a base for their illegal activities. . . ."

"My adorable, insane little girl," cooed Dad. "Go and get dressed. You're going to be late for school."

"Dad, I swear to God . . ."

"Don't swear to God."

"I swear to the Archangel Gabriel . . ."

"Don't swear at all."

"But Daddy, seriously, look at me, I have my serious face on—seriously, the Professor Brothers of Evil have to be arrested. You have to call the police because if I do it they won't believe me. . . ."

"You're right, they won't. Go and put your uniform on."

"But they're the only ones who can tell us where Jenna Jenkins is!"

"Oh, Sophie," sighed Mum, half-smiling. "Everything's fine. We know where Jenna Jenkins is."

My eyeballs almost fell out of their sockets, but I pressed them back in. "What?"

"We received a letter from her this morning. It's just as we suspected—she had a nervous breakdown and left college for a few days to go to London. When she realized everyone was looking for her, she came back and wrote to explain what had happened. She's still shaken up, so she's going to give up on her degree this year and come back next year.

"So you see," said Dad, "there's nothing at all to worry about, my little spinner of funny tales."

Still frowning with incomprehension, I joined Gemma and Toby on the school field.

"What's wrong?" asked Gemma.

"Firstly, PE. Secondly, Jenna Jenkins has mysteriously reappeared. You'll never believe it."

I explained everything to them, and they gaped at the tale of my midnight escapade.

"I don't get it," said Toby eventually. "If Jenna Jenkins says she was in London, who was locked in the cupboard?"

"It can't be anyone else. No one else was missing! Jenna Jenkins is nose-lengtheningly lying in the manner of Pinocchio. She was in that cupboard: I smelt her."

Toby said, tying his shoelaces, "Maybe you

got it all wrong, Sesame. Maybe it wasn't your mum's perfume, just the smell of cleaning products."

"Are you saying my mum smells like a freshly-bleached bathroom?"

"Listen," replied Gemma, "am I the only one who thinks we should drop the case? Whatever happened to her, Jenna Jenkins is now alive and well. Whatever the Professors are doing is their own business. Firstly, it's probably boring, like most businesses. Secondly, they've proven they're not against locking up people in cupboards, and I don't really want to try that out."

"At least," I remarked, "being locked up in a cupboard would give one a good excuse not to go to PE."

Gemma and Toby got up and started warming up for sprint. Mr. Halitosis was already jumping up and down to try to get rid of his beer belly, screaming, "Come on, children! You can do it! You've got it in you!"

"I can't run, Mr. Barnes, I've sprained my ankle."

"A likely story, Sophie! Next time you'll tell me you've injured your ponytail."

"It kind of hurts too, actually."

"Run! Running empties your head."

"That explains it," I muttered.

I ran for about ten minutes, but it didn't empty my head. In fact, my skull was positively purring in the manner of Peter Mortimer when his stomach is being stroked. The overload of mysteries was twisting my brains into plaits.

There was no doubt that the Philips brothers were a criminal couple of crooks. But apart from the fact that one sported a goatee and the other one a moustache, I didn't have any way of proving it to the world. Jenna Jenkins had

said she hadn't been locked up, and if I talked about the dodgy conversation I'd overheard, my parents would choose both not to believe me and to punish me for skating to the Fitz on my own in the middle of the night. Parents are contradictory like that.

"I'm not surprised Professor Philips is a bloodthirsty bandit, anyway," said Toby next to me. "He looked scary."

"Speaking of scary people," interfered Gemma, "what was in his letter to your mum?"

"Dunno . . . I'd completely forgotten about that. Probably something to do with their business meetings."

"I do hope he's better at business than he is

at spelling," said Gemma haughtily.

"What do you—?"

"Sophie Seade, is that what you call running?" Mr. Halitosis's voice interfered.

"Yes, it's a special kind of running I made up. It's much less tiring than normal running."

"I'm afraid someone made it up before you and called it walking. I want to see you run!"

I had to conform to his definition and painfully caught up with Gemma. "What ... do ... you ... mean ... about spelling?"

"Oh, that. Didn't you see? The address on the envelope was riddled with spelling mistakes! Personally, I never get my apostrophes wrong. And I certainly would not leave out the d in 'Cambridge'."

I stopped in my tracks, grabbing Gemma's collar (she gurgled a bit) and stammered, "Spelling mistakes! Oh, Gemz! How did you not tell me that before?"

"I meant to, but then I was gravely ill, remember? Why? It doesn't matter!"

"It does! It does! That's it! I get it!" I

turned to Gemma and Toby. "Reverend Tan told us that Jenna is dyslexic! Professor Philips hadn't written a letter to Mum. He was delivering the letter from Jenna. He forced her to write it!"

"Sophie Seade, if you don't start running again, I'll send you to the Head's!" boomed

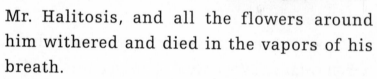

Mr. Halitosis, and all the flowers around him withered and died in the vapors of his breath.

I gave him the furious glare he deserved and started running again, Toby and Gemma on my heels.

"He . . . forced her . . . to write . . . the letter . . . before he let her out of the cupboard—and Mum believed it!"

"Really, Sesame, you're so unfit," said Gemma. "You sound like a tired Labrador."

"I . . . have . . . a stitch . . . " I stopped. "Mr. Barnes, I have a stitch which might very well tear up my stomach if I go on running. Can I stop please?"

"No."

I started again. "Jenna . . . did not have a . . . ouch! a nervous . . . breakdown! She . . . was . . . kidnapped!"

"But why would Professor Philips go through all the trouble if he was going to release her?" asked Toby. "And why didn't she go straight to the police once she was free? It doesn't make sense!"

"How . . . can you speak . . . so smoothly . . . when running? We have . . . to find out what they were up to. . . . Maybe they threatened to kill Jenna . . . if she said anything . . . to the police."

"That's absurd," said Gemma. "No one ever kills anyone in this city. I'm sure it wasn't the same letter. Maybe Professor Philips is dyslexic too!"

"No . . . way! Jenna . . . was forced . . . to write this letter . . . just as I'm being forced . . . to run around this stupid track. And I'll . . . prove it."

But before I could prove it, we had lunch. Well, technically, no one apart from Toby had lunch. We just stared at our plates hungrily and refused to eat. Over in the corner, Mr. Appleyard was looking at his hands a bit meekly.

"Are you sure you're not hungry?" Toby asked, spluttering bits of cabbage. "It's really good!"

"I'm giving my wounded stomach a rest," said Gemma pointedly.

"Yeah, dunno what it was about the Fitz yesterday," retorted Toby. "Must have been bacteria in the air."

Gemma and I threw a dubious glance at him. "Or maybe it was something in the food," she answered pointedly.

"But we only ate my dad's food," remarked Toby, "so it can't have been that."

"Right. By the by, Sesame," said Gemma, "I brought you the new program for the ballet. They reprinted them all without Jenna's name! You'll come and watch it, right? Friday's the first night!"

"Of course, I'd love to," I lied as she rummaged through her bag. "You'll come too, Toby, won't you?"

"I'd rather pull out my own toenails with a pair of rusty pincers," he replied.

"Great. Thanks, Toby," said Gemma. "Look, Sess, here it is."

She handed me the new brochure. Still the same layout on the front page, with that C in a circle—that's where I'd seen it first! What was it doing on Fiona's hoodie and on the Happy Ducks catalogue?

Inside, on the first page, was the same pompous picture of Edwin. And on the next page were a picture and a blurb of the lead, Odette, played by —

"Anastasia Vance?" I looked blankly at Gemma.

"Yeah, apparently, Stacy is just a nickname. Her real name's Anastasia. Bit of a mouthful, I guess, that's why she shortens it."

"Whash you chalking about? Anashtasia?"

Toby intervened, munching on a greyish slice of roast beef. He failed to cut through it with his teeth, so we waited for him to swallow, watching his neck swell up and deflate again in the manner of the boa constrictor gobbling up a small elephant. "I watched it the other day when you abandoned me. You should have stayed with me and watched it too."

"We're talking about a person, not about your smelly film," said Gemma.

"It wasn't smelly! It was well cool! There's this Russian guy who wants to kill everyone— and that girl, Anastasia, doesn't even know she's a princess, and—"

"A princess?" I choked. "A Russian princess?"

"Yes, of course!" exclaimed Toby. "Come on, Sesame, it's the story of that Russian princess, you know? The one that got away when the rest of her family was killed. I'll lend you the DVD. Maybe."

"A Russian princess," I repeated. "A Tsarina. Called Anastasia."

And Gemma and I threw each other a glance which must have been meaningful, because Toby noticed there was something we hadn't told him. So we told 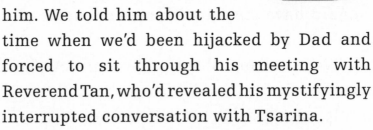 him. We told him about the time when we'd been hijacked by Dad and forced to sit through his meeting with Reverend Tan, who'd revealed his mystifyingly interrupted conversation with Tsarina.

"Illegal activity at her department . . ." repeated Toby. "If that Stacy really is Tsarina, that means it's happening at the computer science department. Look, it's written here on the program—she studies computer science at Trinity College."

This set my sleuthing radar on full blare, and for a good reason, too. "Archie Philips is a professor of computer science at Trinity!" I exclaimed.

"That," said Gemma, "is one funny coincidence."

"But if there's a professor of computer science at her college," whispered Toby, "why would she tell the Chaplain about the thing she'd found out? Why not Archie Philips?"

My sleuthing brain was on autopilot, obligingly slotting the few jigsaw pieces together. "Well, how about because she'd found out *he* was the one doing it? So she had to find someone else to tell it to. And that's not all there is to it. Who do you talk to when you're stuck? Apart from your college Chaplain."

"Your best friend?" asked Gemma.

"Right. Especially when your best friend is also a nosy journalist . . ."

"Jenna Jenkins? You think she told Jenna Jenkins?"

"Well, isn't it a bit strange that Jenna got kidnapped by Ian Philips right after her best friend Stacy found out that Archie Philips was doing something very wrong?"

"That," conceded Gemma, "is one funny bunch of coincidences."

Coincidentally, the subject of that day's English lesson was coincidences.

"Now, children, we're going to talk about coincidences. What's a coincidence? Any idea, Lucas?"

"It's like, when, for example, I think 'Wow, it'd be great if the fire alarm went off and we'd all have to leave the class and have fun outside,' and like, right when I'm thinking about that, it would be a coincidence if the fire alarm . . ."

BRIIIIIIINNNNNNG

" . . . actually went off."

Like just now.

"Right," said Mr. Halitosis, a bit astounded. "Erm . . . OK, everyone, don't run, we're all going downstairs."

After ten fun minutes we were allowed back in the classroom, and Mr. Halitosis, still a bit shaken up, started again. "Right, so Lucas gave us a good example of what a coincidence can be. Any other ideas? Radha?"

"Well, for instance, if I think 'Wouldn't it be a lot of fun if a massive spider dropped from the ceiling right on your head, and . . .'"

"That will be all, thank you," said Mr. Halitosis, throwing nervous glances at the ceiling. "Sophie, can you please give us a definition of a coincidence? Not using examples."

A coincidence. For instance, when a girl is called Anastasia, and somewhere else in town someone is using the screen name Tsarina. For instance, when the same green and white C in a circle keeps popping up in unrelated places. On a duck catalogue. On a ballet brochure. On a T-shirt.

"A coincidence is when, accidentally, two or more things happen at the same time, or seem to be related," I replied.

"That's a fairly good definition," approved Mr. Halitosis. "And when does it stop being a coincidence?"

I shrugged. "Dunno."

"Well, wouldn't you say it stops being a coincidence when you can prove that it didn't happen accidentally, but that the events are related?"

But how do you prove it? I wrote to Toby and Gemma.

You investigate, replied Gemma.

When school finished, I raced up to the city center, flanked on one side by Toby on his bike and on the other by Gemma on her scooter. Destination: Trinity College.

"So the plan is, we find Stacy Vance and pretend that we're her biggest fans ever and that we want our *Swan Lake* program signed,"

I shouted to Gemma. "And then, once we're in the place, we try to find out if she is Tsarina by playing good cop, bad cop!"

"What's good cop, bad cop?" asked Toby, swirling around a taxi.

"It's a police strategy. Gemma pretends to be nice, and I pretend to be mean, and we extract the truth from Stacy Vance in this way."

"And what do *I* do?" he asked indignantly. "You girls are always doing the fun things."

"Well, OK, then, you play fun cop."

"I'm sure it doesn't even exist."

"It does now."

We reached the huge gate of Trinity College. A Porter with a bowler hat was at the door, making sure that a bunch of tourists who wanted to look around the College paid enough money to do so. We dismounted, hid behind the bum of the most gigantic tourist in the group, followed the bum inside, and started investigating the painted name boards at the bottom of students' staircases.

Thankfully, we didn't have to go very far. The

third board we got to simply said:

R1	Miss A. C. Brookland
R2	Mr. E. E. P. Franklin
R3	Mr. P. Mahal
R4	Miss A. Vance

The spiral staircase unrolled under our feet, and we quickly reached R4, which was facing the door to R2.

On to which was pinned, alongside other things, a postcard with a green and white C in a circle.

"What is that C?" I mumbled, and Gemma shrugged.

"Dunno, why?" asked Toby.

"I just—" I said, trying to unpin the postcard from the door, "keep seeing it—everywhere—" and suddenly the door swung open and we were faced with someone I didn't particularly want to see.

"Who's there?" said Edwin.

"My name is Seade—Sesame Seade."

"Ah, I remember you," Edwin groaned. "You were the weird kid at the rehearsal. What are you doing here?"

"Just visiting," I said. I looked over his shoulder. His room was a mess, with all the feathery wings in a pile, and two computers on the desk. "We want Stacy's autograph."

"Children aren't allowed in this staircase."

"We haven't brought our children," I said."Now you're here, can I ask you something?"

He eyed me suspiciously. "What?"

"What does that C mean on your door? The one in the circle?"

He didn't even look. He just laughed and closed the door in my face.

"How rude!" commented Gemma. "He's definitely not a gentleman."

Vengefully, I tried to rip out the C postcard, but then the door behind us opened, and Stacy Vance appeared.

"What's going on?" she said.

She had the most singsong voice I'd ever heard, and was wearing a sort of half-transparent white kimono. If she jumped out of the window she'd probably fly away.

"Honorable dancer," I said, "I'm delighted to meet you. My name is Sesame Seade, and I am your most devoted fan."

"That is not true," said Gemma. "*I* am your most devoted fan. I even enrolled in the orchestra to be able to stare at you every evening."

"No!" exclaimed Toby dramatically, "*I* am your most . . . er . . ." And then he couldn't think of anything else to say, so he went silent. Stacy looked at us, and then around us, as if we were accompanied by invisible parents.

"Can we come in?" I asked.

She nodded. "I guess so. Tea?"

"Yes please."

We walked into a very well-kept room with a lot of white in it, and sat down on a muslin-covered bed, waiting politely until Stacy had boiled the kettle.

"So what brings you here?" she asked, pouring the water into a few mugs.

Gemma got the program out, and Stacy signed it benevolently. While she was doing this, I muttered to Gemma and Toby, "Good cop, bad cop, fun cop!"

Gemma said, "Well, Stacy, I admire you so much. I admire your name. Anastasia . . . it sounds a bit like a Russian princess!"

"In fact," I added threateningly, "it's the name of a Tsarina. And one who's witnessed some seriously illegal activity and won't tell anyone about it. We've got you cornered!"

Smash!

"Oh, I don't like this good cop, bad cop, fun cop thing, Sesame," said Toby. "You made her break her mug.

There's no way I can be fun after that."

Stacy started shivering so much I thought she was going to shatter in millions of pieces. "What's all this about?" she asked. "How the hell do you know about Tsarina?"

"We just overheard a conversation."

"Who?" she questioned anxiously.

"Doesn't matter. They don't know. We figured it out on our own."

"I don't know what you heard," she said, "but it's simply wrong. I was wrong. Tsarina was wrong. There was nothing going on."

"Nothing going on where?"

"At the department. Nothing wrong with any software."

"What software?"

"Wait a minute. What do you know?"

I thought carefully. And then I gave it my best shot.

"We know," I said, "that you found something illegal was going on at the computer science department. Something affecting everyone in this university. The normal thing to do would have been to alert Professor Archie Philips, who's a computer scientist in your college. But you couldn't, because you knew that he was involved in it. You told Jenna Jenkins, who started to investigate the case, and because of that she disappeared. So you started telling Reverend Tan, but the Internet crashed before you could finish. And then," I concluded, "for some reason, you didn't tell anyone else. Maybe because you were afraid that you might disappear as well—just like Jenna."

Stacy's big blue eyes were staring past me, at the door. "I don't know what you're talking about," she articulated. "I was wrong. I thought I'd discovered something, but it turned out to be nothing. I might have told Jenna, but—there was no reason to—to investigate anything."

"Why are you looking at the door?" asked Gemma, and just then the door opened, and Edwin appeared, his brow as knitted as his ugly jumper. He looked at the three of us, and if looks could zap someone to the other side of the solar system, I'd currently be writing this on the chilly side of Pluto. I wondered why he'd come in just to glare at us, especially as it seemed like the only thing he wanted to say was, "Everything all right, Stace?"

"Absolutely," she said.

"Do you know these kids?"

"We're getting to know each other."

He sat down on the floor next to us. "Good," he said. "You should drop by later to try on the adjusted wings, Stacy. They're such good quality, I can't get over how amazing they are. They're not flimsy at all—they're rigid inside, with a real skeleton like a bird's wing! I'm sure they could support the weight of kids like you," he added, looking at us smugly.

"They're definitely a nice *product*, even though sometimes they can get a little *invasive*," replied Stacy coolly.

"That's the kind of high-quality stuff you can buy when you have enough money," Edwin commented.

"Anyway," said Stacy, "I have to get back to work. It was nice meeting you, children. I'm sorry things don't always *compute*, if you see what I mean."

I was starting to wonder why Stacy was talking to us in italics, and apparently Edwin felt a little threatened by it too. "Right, time to go, kids," he said, hurrying us out of the door. "Will you come and see the show?"

"I'm in it," said Gemma. "Playing cello."

"Oh yes," said Edwin, and he winced.

Product. Invasive. Compute.

I wasn't sure what was going on, but I knew we had to talk to Jeremy Hopkins about it.

But as we left Trinity College, Gemma got a call on her mobile from her mum who was parked on a double yellow line outside the shopping center and could Gemma please hurry up and meet her there or else!

"See you tomorrow," said Gemma mournfully. "Let me know how the investigation goes."

"So it's just you and me, Toby," I said. "We'll solve this mystery together! Toby?"

But Toby was pulling at his hair, staring at what I first thought was nothing at all on a nearby railing, until I got closer and realized it was a cleanly sawn open bike lock.

"Can you believe it? My bike got stolen again!"

"Isn't it the third time this year?"

"It's the fourth! I've got to go home, Sesame. I'm not allowed to walk back after five o'clock."

"But cycling is fine?"

"Yes, because I go too fast to get kidnapped."

Parents have weird rules.

"OK," I said, "I'll be brave and continue to investigate on my own. Sorry about your bike, Toby."

"I'd called it Victor," he snivelled.

"You shouldn't have bothered. It's a fact of life that you can't get attached to bikes in Cambridge. They always get nicked."

Upon which I bid farewell to poor Toby and skated off.

"Knock knock!"

Fiona was in her room, reading an enormous book in bed.

"Hi, Sesame. How did last night's expedition go?"

"Bizarrely. And now I need to find Jeremy Hopkins. And for that I'm going to need the great web of knowledge."

"An encyclopedia?"

"No, Facebook, of course. Could you look up his college for me, please?"

"Sure." She switched on her computer and waited for it to load. "But what's left to investigate? Jenna's reappeared."

"Mysteriously reappeared," I politely corrected her.

"Nothing mysterious about it. Don't look so dejected—I'm sure one day you'll find a nice juicy sleuthing case with murders in it."

"This one might still have murders in it! Jenna Jenkins might not be safe!"

Fiona laughed. "She's just up the river, in Grantchester. No one gets murdered there."

Now this was news to me, as I'd thought the evasive ballerina was a Londoner. "What's she doing in Grantchester?"

"Her grandma lives there, in a little pink cottage on the river. Jenna's staying with her. I guess after her breakdown, she needed some peace and quiet." She clicked the Internet icon. "She must have been more fragile than she looked."

"But Jeremy Hopkins told me Jenna Jenkins wasn't fragile, that she wasn't the kind of person who would—Wait! What's that on the screen? What is that thing?"

"What? Calm down, that's just the new Internet start page for the college."

"But that C! That green and white C in the circle! What is it?"

Fiona looked a bit bemused. "Don't tell me you've never seen it before."

"Are you joking, I've seen it way too much recently! What is it?"

"God, Sesame, you live a shielded life, don't you? It's the Cooperture logo, of course."

VIII

Ten minutes later, I was inside Gonville & Caius College. The trees shattered sunlight on the ground, and I got distracted for a while by the sprinklers on the lawn. How can you not stand in their sprinkling range? I don't understand how adults resist the urge. It's not even as if I had a choice. I have to stand under the sprinkler. Maybe I'm actually a plant? Looking at the Porter on duty, he seemed to think I was more some kind of weed.

"Knock knock!"

I don't think I'd ever knocked on so many student doors in a single day.

"Who's there?"

"Sesame Seade, at your service."

The door opened slightly and an eye belonging to Jeremy Hopkins became visible. This eye eyed me, and then the door opened completely to allow the second eye in the pair to look at me too.

"Sesame, what a good surprise! I hope your father knows you're here."

"Of course," I said, which wasn't exactly a lie because he's always in touch with Someone Who Knows Everything. "Can I come in?"

The funny thing about Jeremy's room was that I never came in direct contact with the floor. Not because the room had zero gravity but because the floor was covered in clothes and books and papers and strange objects. I closed my eyes politely to avoid noticing a very big pile of dirty laundry with a fly buzzing lazily around it.

"OK," said Jeremy. "How far are you in your investigation, young sleuth? Have you found any odd buttons or sweet wrappers?"

"Let's start at the very beginning. It's a very good place to start. You know Jenna's reappeared, right?"

"Yes. She won't answer my calls, though."

"Do you believe in the breakdown theory?"

"No."

"Me neither. I think Jenna was kidnapped and then released. And that it has everything to do with Cooperture Ltd."

"What?" laughed Jeremy as if I'd said it had everything to do with the President of the United States of America.

"Don't laugh! The Cooperture people have given hundreds of thousands of pounds to lots of different colleges, and it was Professor Ian Philips who put the College Heads in touch with them. Oh, yes, and while we're on this subject, you might also be interested to know that Ian

Philips kidnapped Jenna Jenkins."

And I told him everything I knew, watching with curiosity as his jaw dropped and eyes widened in the amusing manner of a cartoon character. Since I was doing so well at captivating my audience, I ended my revelation with a flourish: "Additionally, Edwin also sends my sleuthing radar beeping—why, in his presence, does Stacy behave like a rabbit trapped in the headlights of an oncoming heavyweight? Does he know that she knows? And even if he does, why would he care?"

"If Cooperture's really involved in this affair from start to finish, that's easily explained," said Jeremy.

"Why?"

"Edwin Franklin's the son of Rudolph Franklin, the President of Cooperture. That's why the C is all over the brochure for *Swan Lake*. Cooperture are sponsoring the show."

"Mr. Franklin! Yes, Mum introduced him to me in Auntie's Tea Shop! That's why Edwin's face seemed familiar. And that's why he had a promotional postcard of Cooperture on his door. And that's where he got the money to put on such a big show. . . ."

"And there's something else. The show's brochure said that Edwin Franklin is a Classicist."

"He's not classy at all. He dresses like my great-grandfather would if he was color-blind."

"Not classy, you loony—a Classicist. Someone who studies Greek and Latin."

"Greek and Latin? Just like . . ."

"That's right, just like your dear Professor Ian Philips. And in the same college."

"Wow. Coincidence! Edwin and Mr. Franklin, Ian Philips and Archie Philips. Seems like these four people might know one another pretty well."

"Blimey," sighed Jeremy, crossing his hands under his head. "Sesame, you're a star. Can't believe you found all that on your own."

"Oh please, don't praise me. Couldn't have done it without my brain."

"There's just one problem."

"What is it?"

"We simply have no idea what it is that the

Professors Philips and Cooperture are doing that's illegal. If Stacy and Jenna won't talk, how are we going to find out?"

"I suggest we go for a walk," I said. "It helps me to see things clearly. Dogs do it all the time."

In fact I was looking forward to going outside because of the sprinkler, of course. But as we walked out of the building, three nasty surprises were awaiting us. Firstly, the sprinkler had been turned off and was sitting there like an upturned steel spider. Secondly, my dad was standing next to it, looking wet. Thirdly, my dad was standing next to it, looking furious.

"Sophie Margaret Catriona Seade!"

I rolled my eyes.

"Jeremy Hopkins!"

Jeremy Hopkins turned a pale shade of gray.

"That sprinkler!"

A gardener raking some leaves on the side coughed a bit awkwardly.

"Hello, Reverend Seade!" I said warmly, because I sensed that the atmosphere was a little tense. Dad crossed the lawn, his cassock dripping, and stopped right in front of us, clearly struggling to decide which of the many annoying things in his life he should deal with first.

He finally settled on the following order: 1) sprinkler; 2) Jeremy Hopkins; 3) me.

"That sprinkler!" he shouted. "It looked like it was off! It wasn't sprinkling a molecule of water until I happened to walk past it!"

"I think, Daddy, that we can all learn something from this experience, and

that is . . ."

"Jeremy Hopkins! What are you doing here, Jeremy Hopkins?"

"This is my college," replied Jeremy Hopkins.

"What are you doing with my daughter again?"

"Well, she came to my room, and we were about to take a walk outside to clear our minds."

"She came to your room?" Dad repeated.

I put a calming hand on his wet shoulder. "No need to worry, perfectly protective Papa," I said soothingly. "Jeremy and I are friends."

"Come on, Reverend," said Jeremy Hopkins, "I'm nineteen years old. Sesame's just a kid. She probably sees me as a very old man."

"Not to mention that his clothes are filthy!" I commented, a bit more loudly than I'd planned (making six tourists, two Porters and the gardener glance at us weirdly). Jeremy, I think, seemed a tad uncomfortable. On the plus side, Dad was getting drier, since the water on his cassock was evaporating quickly in the heat of his anger.

"Sophie," he said, "your mother and I had no

idea where you were. We had to watch the CCTV recordings in College that showed us that you'd been to Fiona Lumley's room, who then told us you'd gone to Gonville & Caius. Do you have any idea how worried we were?"

"No, Daddy."

"You are an impossible, incontrollable, incomprehensible little . . . little . . . little . . ."

"Girl?" said the gardener.

"No," said Dad, "a little . . ."

"Sweetheart?" said a tourist.

"No," said Dad, "a little . . ."

"Angel?" said a student.

"Certainly not!" said Dad. "You're a little demon, Sophie! A little juvenile delinquent! A little domestic tyrant!"

"She doesn't look it," said a woman who started patting my head.

"I'm really not, Madam," I whined. "It all comes from a big problem in my life."

"What is it, my dear?" asked the woman and all the other people who had gathered around.

"I don't have a mobile phone," I said. "If I had

a mobile phone, like Toby and Gemma and Lucas and Eugenie, I'd be able to call my parents and tell them what I'm up to. But they don't want me to have one!"

"Oh!" everyone exclaimed.

"For goodness sake!" cried Dad. "What is this, some kind of public trial? Come, Sophie."

"Bye, Jeremy!"

"Bye, Sesame!"

"Bye, everyone!"

"Bye, Sesame!"

And I was dragged out of Gonville & Caius.

I was given a slap on the bum, even though that's forbidden by the European Union, and sent to my room with fifty pages of the Bible to read, and not even fun ones with murders. Thankfully, Peter Mortimer was around to interrupt my reading by collapsing unexpectedly on the Book to get stroked.

At half past nine, the door opened, and Mum came in with a plate of sandwiches. Behind her was Dad, who was carrying a cup of tea.

"Dinner," grumbled Mum.

"I am most obliged," I said trying to be nice.

They both sat down on my bed. "You know, it's not fun for us to punish you," Dad stated.

"Please don't feel like you have to," I said benevolently.

"Listen, Sophie. We've thought long and hard about that mobile phone thing."

"Oh, Daddy! Please don't mention it."

"We do think that it would be less stressful for us if we knew that you were carrying a phone."

"I don't care about the phone. Just say you've forgiven me."

"We have forgiven you. But about the phone . . ."

"No, dearest parents, I don't want to talk about the phone. I've been very naughty."

"You have," confirmed Mum. "However, having thought about the phone, we think it would be better if you did have one . . ."

"I don't think so, Mummy. It's very bad for a child as young as me to have a phone."

"Hush! We're not asking you if you want a phone, we're telling you that you *shall* have a phone!" interrupted Dad. "Whether you like it or not!"

"Oh, all right then."

"In fact," Mum added, "I was thinking about it only yesterday, and looked for phones online. We'll go to the shops tomorrow."

"You will have the simplest phone with no Internet access," declared Dad, "and no camera."

"Does that still exist?"

Mum looked at Dad, who looked at Mum. "I'm sure it does," said Mum, sounding unsure. "Anyway, we'll go tomorrow. Say *yes, Mummy*."

"Yes, Mummy."

"Good night, then."

"The problem with Sophie is that she's a reluctant little Aliboron," said Dad as they closed the door.

As soon as their footsteps had faded away down the staircase, I leapt out of the window and on to the little terrace, slid down my tree, and roller-skated till the city was just a brown blur of gargoyles, bikes and railings under the sandy streetlamps.

There was one person in the world I absolutely wanted to meet.

Well, two people. J.K. Rowling first, always. And then Jenna Jenkins. Whose address I knew by heart:

Jenna Jenkins
Little pink cottage on the river
Grantchester

Only she could detangle the big knot of Cs and swans and money and explain the mysterious not-kidnapping and release. If I could get her to speak, I'd understand everything.

There are four ways to get to Grantchester. Firstly, you can drive there. But I haven't got my driving licence yet. Secondly, you can skate there. But I didn't have my wrist protections on so it would have been dangerous. Thirdly, you can fly there in the manner of Superman. But as mentioned before, I never asked for such superpowers when I decided to become Cambridge's number one supersleuth.

Fourthly, you can sail there. And for that, you need a ship. And I knew exactly where to find a ship.

So there I was, in the middle of the night, carrying a canary-yellow canoe on my back in the manner of the armadillo.

"Water, water everywhere!" I chanted as I dropped the canoe in the river. I then lowered myself into the wobbly vessel, put on a life jacket and grabbed the paddle.

The Greek-statue-man had been right. It was the easiest craft to steer in marine history. You just plunged one side of the paddle in the water on the right of the canoe, like this—and then on the other side, like that—and it raced upstream in the manner of wild salmon.

"Grantchester, here I come! I shall discover

your heretofore undiscovered lands, and name them Sesamia!"

The night was a black bell splattered with stars. On the banks of the river, the grass grew thick and tangled, and croaked "ribbit ribbit" when the glistening ripples of water reached it. Sometimes the black water plopped at me, and as I reached the heretofore undiscovered banks of Grantchester an immense white owl descended like a ghost on the river and snatched a fish that no one else had noticed. It was a wild world.

But gradually I started seeing houses again, and the night became lighter. I'd reached the village. Sitting quietly at the bottom of their little gardens, the cottages of Grantchester appeared, some of them still broken by squares of yellow light or the stormy bluish glow of a television.

One problem with the night is that everything looks gray in it. Yellow looks gray; red looks gray; try blue, it also looks gray; gray looks very gray; even white looks gray; and pink, unfortunately, also looks gray.

I had no way of telling a pink cottage from a neon-yellow one.

"Another very disorganized mission," I scolded myself as I stopped paddling to scratch my chin. "I'm not a very good sleuth."

"Quack."

"Why, I wouldn't go as far as to say I'm a quack, thank you very much."

"Quack."

"This is getting insulting!"

"Quack."

I looked around to face my detractor.

And ended up nose to beak with the pregnant duck.

✫✫✫

Now, that's the part when most people will say I'm lying or wrong, that it wasn't the same pregnant duck as the one I'd saved and shared strawberry sweets with. Let me get this straight. I have no scientific evidence that it actually was my pregnant duck. I didn't do a DNA test or take her fingerprints. But look at it this way. I can't see any valid reason why any other duck than the one I saved from the claws of Peter Mortimer would have helped me on my mission. If you can think of a valid reason, let me know at this address:

Sesame Seade
Master's Lodge
Christ's College
Cambridge CB2 3BU
UK

So my pregnant duck quacked at me, and I was so happy to see her I quacked back, which surprised her a little. And then she joyously went on swimming, her little tail waggling from left to right like Mum's forefinger when she says "Don't do this, Sophie." I followed her, searing through the black waters. A few minutes later she stopped in front of a pretty little back garden and jumped out of the water on to the mooring platform.

I heaved myself on to the bank—my lower

body still inside the canoe—and crawled on the grass where I struggled out of the boat in the manner of the hermit crab leaving its shell for a bigger one. I hid the canoe and the paddle behind a big bush of reeds and walked up to the back of cottage in my socks. The house was mostly dark, but one of the top floor windows was bathed in milky white light. I climbed on a compost bin and

lifted myself up on the bow-window. The duck quacked at me in encouragement. The soft light from inside the house poured on to the window sill, painting it back to its daytime color—pink.

I carefully folded my finger and, with the tip of the first knuckle, tapped the glass three short times.

Inside, something ruffled.

I tapped another three short times.

Inside, something shuffled.

I tapped another three short times.

Inside, something scuffled.

And suddenly the sash-window slid up, and I was dragged inside by powerful hands, which pulled me to a powerful chest, holding a powerful sword right under my little neck!

(It was actually Jenna's quite small hands, pulling me to her quite skinny chest, holding a pen-knife. But in the heat of the action, it feels much scarier.)

"Who are you?" she hissed.

"Sesame Seade," I hissed back (my name is easily hissed).

"What are you doing here?"

"I want to talk to you."

"Who sent you?"

"No one. No one. Certainly not Cooperture."

She let go of me and turned me around. "You're just a kid," she observed, a bit baffled. "How did you get here?"

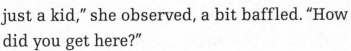

"I canoed up the Cam."

Now I was inside, I could see where the white light came from—a phone on the desk. There was no other light switched on in the bedroom, which was a sweet little cottage bedroom with many flower patterns.

Jenna Jenkins sat on the bed and sighed. "I'm not even surprised. I have no idea what's going on these days."

"I've come to ask you about this whole affair,"

I said, sitting down cross-legged on the floor. "I know lots of things about what happened, but some pieces of the jigsaw are still missing."

"What do you know?"

"You never went to London. You were kidnapped by Professor Ian Philips and his brother, Archie Philips, and spent three days in a broom cupboard at the Fitzwilliam Museum."

Her eyes widened, but she didn't say anything.

I went on, "Stacy Vance, your best friend, discovered that something fishy was going on at the computer science department—something which Archie Philips was involved in. She told you, and you started investigating the case for *UniGossip*. You found out that it had all to do with Cooperture's plans to smother Cambridge colleges in banknotes, helped by Ian Philips who organized the meetings. And you were about to tell Jeremy Hopkins about it when you suddenly vanished. Three days later, you reappeared like nothing had happened and faked depression. As for Stacy, she's now pretending there wasn't anything weird going on at all, and planning to spend the end of the week cheerfully skipping across a stage in a tatty tutu."

Jenna was just looking at her fingers. I waited for her to speak, and finally she simply said, "What don't you know?"

"Well, for a start, I don't know what Cooperture and the Philipses have actually done that's so wrong that they need to convert a broom cupboard into a dark dungeon to lock up anyone who might have found out. Secondly, I don't know how they managed to kidnap you. I also don't know how you found out Cooperture were involved. Finally, I don't know why you didn't go straight to the police after being released by Professor Philips—if he truly released you, that is, and you didn't run away."

"You're not a bad sleuth, you know?" she mumbled. "OK, I'll answer some of your questions. It all started one evening when Stacy decided to have a bit of fun breaking into password-protected parts of the computer science department's network. She stumbled upon a piece of very suspicious software belonging to Archie Philips. She saw immediately that it wasn't anything legal. And she decided to tell me about it."

"Why tell you and not the police?"

"Well, see, she was stuck. Firstly, she'd found it illegally—it's not exactly OK to break into protected bits of a network. But also, she didn't know if Archie had been working on it for the wrong reasons, or if it was just an exercise in programming. So I decided to investigate. I went to the department to spy on Archie Philips, and after a while I overheard a phone conversation between him and someone else. Archie said that the software was now ready, and that his job stopped there—it was now the task of the other person, the one he was calling, to get Cooperture in touch with the colleges."

"Ian Philips! His brother."

"Yes. I guessed that when he said 'Daddy would be proud of us!' before hanging up."

"Sounds like a pleasant kind of family."

"From there, it was easy enough to find Ian

Philips. Since he seemed to be the one who'd organized the whole project—he was the brain, and Archie the hands, if that makes sense—I phoned Ian. I told him everything I knew. Very smoothly and politely, he convinced me to come and meet him at the Museum. I arrived, he asked me to wait a minute in that little room. And then he simply closed the door on me. It wasn't even a proper abduction."

"Why did he do it?"

"Because he didn't want me around when Cooperture came. He and his brother kept me there until they'd left and all the deals were done and all the money had gone through."

"Why didn't you just scream? If you could chomp on McVitie's, you could have screamed."

"No, I had good reasons to keep quiet and just wait for my release. Let's say we'd started to negotiate my silence."

"Negotiate? What do you mean?"

"Right, I think you're in need of good advice ... Sesame, is that right? Sesame, I have no idea how you gathered so much information about this whole thing, but I seriously recommend you forget everything about it. They persuaded me to forget everything about it, too."

"Persuade you? How did they persuade you?"

She laughed sombrely. "When you've got that sort of money, it's easy to persuade a student who's got a £90,000 debt and a brother in need of private care. When you've got that sort of money, there's nothing you can't buy. Not even silence."

"But what is it that they've done? Tell me —what is it that they don't want anyone to find out?"

"I thought you'd seen Stacy. She knows more or less what's going on, even though she didn't know it was linked to Cooperture until I found it out."

"She wouldn't tell me anything about it."

"Of course she wouldn't. If she opened her mouth, not only would she be in big trouble, but the show would also collapse. And Edwin would drag her name through the mud on the national ballet scene. And she's very keen to become a professional ballerina, Stacy is."

"Well, if she won't tell me, you'll have to—what is it that they've done?"

"No, I'm sorry," she said, firmly shaking her head. "I can't. That's the price I paid for my release."

"Is Archie Philips involved in it? Or just his brother?"

"Let's not play riddles," she replied.

"Is it really illegal?"

"Perfectly illegal."

"Is anyone going to die?"

"No, it's not like that. Listen, I said I didn't want to play riddles!" she moaned, getting up. "It's not like that—it's not death, it's not drugs, it's not that kind of violence. I wouldn't let it happen if it was that."

"So you think it's not a very serious matter?"

"I think," she said carefully, "it's not serious enough for me to reject an offer like the one they made me." She walked around the room, checked her phone nervously. "I've said way too much already. I'll stop here. Sorry to disappoint."

I stayed there another ten minutes, nagging her with questions—I thought I'd had years of practice with my parents—but it was as if her lips had been sealed with a C in a circle. Eventually, I gave up.

"Right. I'll see myself out."

"Suit yourself. And believe me, Sesame—I don't think you'll ever find out what's actually going on, but if you ever do—just let it go, OK? Don't think about it. It's not worth putting yourself at risk for something that doesn't put anyone in actual danger."

"Then what . . .?"

"Just go."

I climbed over the window sill, leapt down to the moist grass, and went to fetch my canoe and paddle. When I looked back, I saw Jenna's face at the window in the dusty white light. I waved to her, but she just closed the window and turned off her phone. The whole cottage went black.

"Quack."

"You're still here?"

The pregnant duck accompanied me all the way back to Cambridge. Maybe as a mum-to-be she felt a bit protective of me. Or maybe she was just going back to Emmanuel College. I took the canoe, paddle and life jacket back into the hangar and put my roller skates on. The city was entirely asleep, and skating back I felt like I'd never been so loud in my life. Thankfully, no one opened their windows to check where the thundering noise came from. Even the gargoyles were slumbering instead of guarding the colleges.

There was no police car in front of Christ's, so I assumed my parents hadn't discovered I was gone, for which I thanked whoever was in charge. I kicked off my roller skates, climbed up the tree, collapsed into bed, and dreamt of swans.

IX

When I stumbled into the living-room in the morning, Mum and Dad were emitting lots of wows and ahs. Assuming reasonably that they were meant for me, I said "Oh please, parents, don't, it's a bit embarrassing," but I then realized that they were both looking at something on a table which was neither me nor a picture of me.

"Ah, Sophie! Look at that," said Mum. "We've just received a catalogue of a new range of mobile phones called Phone4Kidz!"

"Phone4Kidz?" I repeated, horror-struck.

"Look: phones which are especially designed for children like you! 'No nasties in these kid-friendly phones that will keep your child in check and leave you worry-free!' That's just what we need."

I threw a disbelieving glance at the catalogue. The phones looked like walkie-talkie toys for three-year-olds. One of them only had four buttons: a green phone-shaped one to receive a call, a pink one with an M to "Call Mummy," a blue one with a D to "Call Daddy," and a black car-shaped one to "Call the police."

"Right, darling," said Mum, "we'll pick you up after school and take you to the Carphone Warehouse. Apparently they sell some of these phones . . ." she shuffled through the catalogue. "Yes, they do. And then we'll have tea at Auntie's! Just the three of us. It'll be fun! What a lovely coincidence that we got this catalogue today of all days!"

She babbled on about it, but it was as if her voice was coming from a distant galaxy. My brain had plucked one word out of her speech. Coincidence.

As she slapped the catalogue back on the table, I noticed the green and white C in a circle.

Coincidence.

Heavily, I turned the catalogue around.

Phone4Kidz are proud to be marketed by Cooperture Ltd, London.

"Mum," I said in a voice that was ridiculously high-pitched, "did you say you looked up mobile phones on the Internet the other day?"

"Yes, I did a quick search."

"From here? From the College's Internet?"

"Yes, why?"

"Which keywords did you type in?"

"Can't remember, darling."

"I'm sure you can remember if you squeeze your eyelids shut and stick out your tongue like this, look . . ."

Mum tried (she was in a good mood). "Oh yes, I typed something in the way of 'Mobile phones suitable for children.' But I didn't look for very long, and we don't need to worry about it now anyway. Get ready, darling, you're leaving in half an hour. . . . What are you doing?"

"Writing."

"Writing what?"

"A letter."

"Is this really the right time? You haven't

even showered yet!"

"Sorry, have to do it now."

"Who are you writing to?"

"Leave her alone, Agnes, she's allowed to have her little secrets," chided Dad, craning his neck like an ostrich to look at what I was writing.

But I'd finished. Swiftly, I folded the letter in three, slipped it in an envelope, and went and hid in the toilet to write the address:

Jeremy Hopkins
Gonville & Caius College

I then ran to the Porters' Lodge to drop the letter in the intra-university post box. It would reach Jeremy this very morning. Then he would know everything I knew. And he would run to the police and they would believe him (no one ever believes me, because apparently I have a considerable track record of lying).

The last piece of the jigsaw had finally slotted into place.

What Cooperture Ltd had asked colleges to install on their Internet servers wasn't just an ad—oh, far from it—that was just what they'd told colleges. It was actually a spy—a piece of software that tracked all activity on computers to find customers for their brands. Hundreds of students and staff members were being spied on by Cooperture at this very moment— their activities filed, their tastes analyzed. And catalogues, adverts and promotional products were sent according to them.

That was why Fiona the medicine student was now parading around with a medicine-themed hoodie! That was why the Happy Ducks catalogue had waddled its way through our front door just after Dad had researched ducks online! That was why the fatal flyer for farcical phones had fallen out of the heavens into my parents' hands! All brought to you courtesy of Cooperture. Ka-ching! It was easy to see how Cooperture would quickly earn back all the dosh they'd dished out, and much more.

The C in the circle was everywhere, like a

little green eye, spying on all of us. Because of it, everyone in the university had become Cooperture's prey. Because of it, Jenna Jenkins had had to give up on being a journalist, a ballerina, and a student. Because of it, my parents were going to buy me a phone that would make the entire world howl with laughter.

And I was pretty sure all of these, especially the last, were completely illegal.

"They'll all rot in a rat-infested gaol!" I promised the College crest as I passed the gate.

Not enough of a punishment.

"They'll all be hanged by the feet above a caiman-infested pool!" I promised the statue of Henry VIII as I passed by King's College.

Still wasn't enough of a punishment.

"Their eyes will be nibbled on alive by a horde of poisonous red ants while a goat licks their feet with her sandpaper-like tongue!" I promised the thousand bikes aligned inside Peterhouse College.

And then I shook my fist at the Fitzwilliam Museum, inside which the two brothers were probably drinking champagne to their success.

I was going to tell Toby and Gemma everything about my stupendous findings, but unexpectedly, I had to deal with two other problems.

Firstly, Gemma: "I'm completely stressed out about tomorrow's performance. What if I get it all wrong? What if I forget how to play, how to speak, how to breathe, what if I throw up all over my cello? What if someone falls into the pit right on to my head?"

Secondly, Toby: "Guess what! My dad's been asked to prepare the buffet for the party after the show! It's going to be awesome! Oh, I'm still not coming to the show, though. I'd rather eat a purée of my own bowels with chopped tarragon."

"OK, first things first: Gemz, everything's going to be all right. You're the Picasso of cello-playing. Everyone will give you a standing ovation at the end. In fact they'll ask you to sign their bare chests after the show. Second things second: Toby, what's that about? What after-party?"

"Well, after tomorrow's performance people will be heading to the art gallery at the corner of Jesus Lane and Sidney Street."

"I don't know street names."

"The art gallery that had a painting of a naked man in the window last month."

"Oh, yes, that one!" (Mum and Dad kept

finding excuses to go another route while that naked man was still in the window.)

"Anyway, there'll be a party there to celebrate the first night of the show! Dad's been asked to organize the buffet. He's being paid a lot for it!"

"I bet," I said somberly. I thought I could guess who was paying him.

"You can come as my guest, Sesame," said Gemma. "It'll be fun! And you know what? Professor Philips will be there! I saw his name on the list. He's a guest of Edwin's dad."

"Yes, I'll come along. I'll definitely come along. Right. Will you listen to me now?"

They listened intently, and I told them the whole story. Twice, since Toby didn't get the idea the first time, but even then he said, "I can't see what's wrong with getting adverts for things you actually like, as opposed to adverts for snow tires or stair lifts," and Gemma had to say, "Toby. Trust us. It's not good."

"Anyway, keep it quiet," I warned them. "Don't go and trumpet it around the galaxy like it's public knowledge. If the Professors learn that we've found them out, they'll escape to the South American jungle and will never be found again! I've written to Jeremy to tell him to go to the police. I know he's only a student, but he's eight years older than us, so they'll believe him eight times more."

Toby and Gemma promised to keep quiet, and the school bell drilled nicely through our ears.

In French class the most incredible and unexpected thing happened.

There was a knock on the door. (That wasn't the incredible bit.)

"Entrez!" said the French teaching assistant, Mademoiselle Corentin.

The door opened, and Mrs. Appleyard *entra*.

"Hello," said Mrs. Appleyard, looking a bit bemused. "I . . . er . . . have a letter for Sesame Seade."

"Une lettre?" repeated Mademoiselle Corentin. *"Pour mademoiselle Seade?"*

"Er . . . *oui*," Mrs. Appleyard assumed. "A young man just dropped by to give it to her."

"*Un jeune homme vient de passer pour vous la lui donner?*" said Mademoiselle Corentin.

"Right," Mrs. Appleyard guessed. "Apparently it's urgent."

"*Apparemment c'est urgent?*" said Mademoiselle Corentin.

"Here it is, anyway," retorted Mrs. Appleyard who was visibly getting tired of the conversation.

"*La voilà donc*," Mademoiselle Corentin translated. "*Mademoiselle Seade! Une lettre pour vous.*"

"*Merci* very much!" I replied, grabbing the envelope.

The whole class was gaping at me as if I'd just received a letter from Hogwarts. It was addressed to Sesame Seade, Goodall School. I walked back to my seat and ripped the envelope open under the disapproving eye of Mademoiselle Corentin, who went back to telling us about the word for "camembert."

Hi Sesame,

Thanks for your letter. Amazing. I can hardly believe it—you've found them out! Listen—I can't go to the police, it doesn't work like that. I have to get a confession from Ian Philips first. I'll go to see him today. I'll make him talk and then get back to you tonight. We'll frame him!

Speak soon, call me if you need to.

Jeremy x

Inside was a phone number and a short note:

This was huge news. Not only had I received a secret message in the middle of French class, but it was from a boy and had an x at the end. I could have swooned if I'd been a bit of a ninny. I showed it to Toby and Gemma and they did thumbs-up like maniacs.

Right. Do you want to come over to my house after school? Toby wrote in the margin of his exercise book.

Can't, I replied in felt-tip on my eraser, **my parents are coming to pick me up to** (there I ran out of space and wrote the rest on my hand) **buy a mobile phone.**

At last! exclaimed Gemma on last week's French test. **Which one are you getting?**

A disastrously disgusting one, I pencilled on the desk, wiping it with my left hand as I went along as Mademoiselle Corentin would bulldoze me to absolute flatness if she saw me. **One of the Phone4Kidz range!**

HAHAHA! Toby and Gemma wrote.

Don't be too sad, Gemma added. **They have cool alphabet games!**

I collapsed on the desk in profound misery.

At four o'clock, to add to the intensely humiliating life I was already living, Mum and Dad were waiting outside the school gates with open arms and exclamations of "Yoo-hoo! Sophie!"

"Good afternoon, parents. No need to hold my hand. I trust you've had a nice day."

"What's that on your hand?" chimed Dad. "Buy a mobile phone—isn't she sweet! As if it was her responsibility!"

"Look, here we are!" exclaimed Mum. "The Carphone Warehouse! Super cool!"

"Please, Mum, no 'super cools'."

"Hello-o-o!" Dad sang to a salesman who looked like he was only a few weeks older than me. "We're looking for a mobile phone for our little girl."

"Less of the little, please," I implored.

"Our range of phones is there, we have this new smartphone with 3D video calls . . ."

"Tut-tut," Mum tut-tutted. "We know what we want." And she produced the Phone4Kidz catalogue. I retreated into a corner in the manner of a hibernating hamster and covered my red face with my hands.

"Are you sure?" the salesman asked. "They're really bare, these phones—no applications, no time-fillers . . ."

"Time-fillers!" Dad snorted. "That is the problem with your generation, young man—instead of using time productively, you just fill it!"

"This is torture," I informed a baby in a pram right next to me.

"Right," said the salesman, throwing a sad glance at me, "here's the Phone4Kidz range."

Mum and Dad browsed through the accursed collection, marvelling at their complete lack of functions, except for ...

"Isn't this clever! A timer for tooth-brushing!"

"And this, look! An alphabet game!"

"You can also record a three-minute message on the phone," said the salesman, "stating your address and phone number for instance, which your daughter can play to adults if she gets lost."

"Wow!"

I started to hope for a nuclear bomb to be dropped on Cambridge by a rival university. Before it could happen, though, Mum and Dad decided this was their absolute favorite phone, ensured that I liked  it by asking me to confirm that I liked it, and parted with £25 plus a £10 top-up to be able to leave the shop with their new treasure.

After dinner, I still hadn't heard back from Jeremy, so I went to hide under my duvet to call him from my ridiculous new phone. The ringtone went on for a long time, until Jeremy's tired voice emerged at the end of the line.

"Hello? Who's this?'"

"It's me, Sesame."

"Oh. Sesame. Hi."

"Are you OK?"

"Yes. Why? Do I sound not-OK?"

"Dunno. A little bit. So?"

"So what?

"How did your meeting with Professor Philips go?"

"Oh, that." He sighed deeply.

"Yes, that!"

"Yeah . . . Listen, Sesame. Er . . . I think we should just drop it, all right?"

"What do you mean? What did he say?"

"Lots of things. It's too complicated for you to understand. Anyway. Have you had a nice day? What are you up to?"

"Wait a minute," I said. "What's going on?" Did he confess? Are you going to denounce him to the police?"

"Well, no. No point. Listen, Sess . . . It's too difficult for you to get your mind around these things, you know, but . . . Trust me, right? We're dropping the case."

And suddenly I understood, and it was as if I'd swallowed a chip of flint stone.

"He paid you," I croaked. "He paid you, like he did with Jenna! He bought your silence!"

"No, it's not like that, Sesame. You're being too dramatic."

"Jeremy, you can't do this! You have to tell the police!"

"It's a fair enough deal, when you think about it. Colleges get money to pay for better things for the students. Cooperture get their money back when people buy their clients' products. And Professor Philips gets paid for putting the two in touch."

"No," I choked, "seriously, you can't take his money . . ."

"I'm not technically taking his money. He's paying back my student debt and helping me get on to a great journalism course. It's a lot when you're just starting out in life, you know."

"No, Jeremy, listen to me—it's not right!"

"Who knows what's right?" he groaned. "Don't judge me, Sesame. You'd do the same if you were me. You would."

He said a soft "bye," and hung up.

X

The Professor brothers of evil and the Cooperture terrorists of computer invasion would never rot in a rat-infested gaol. I was so dejected I didn't even laugh when Peter Mortimer dropped a dead moth in Dad's pea soup.

The next gloomy morning, I woke up gloomily, got dressed gloomily, ate breakfast gloomily, and was gloomily driven to school in the Smurfmobile.

"You look a bit gloomy," Dad remarked. "Have you got toothache?"

"It would only be right," I replied sourly, "after brushing them like a fanatic for three whole minutes with my phone timer."

"That little musical piece is quite fun," Dad chuckled.

It was, in fact, so bad that I'd spent the three minutes of tooth-brushing praying for human-eating aliens to hook me out of the bathroom and into the turquoise sky.

As we reached school, Dad pointed a warning forefinger at my nose:

"Don't get your phone stolen!"

"No risk of that, unless the nuttiest of thieves in the whole world happens to be roaming the premises."

I'd hoped Toby and Gemma would share my indignation at Jeremy's act of high treason, but Toby still didn't really get why the Professors had done anything wrong and Gemma was so stressed about that evening's first performance of *Swan Lake* that her whole body was just a blur. There was no way I could get her to think that more tragic things were happening in our little city. Eventually, I gave up.

"You'll be all right," I said to her seven hundred times that day, to which she replied something different each time:

"I might sneeze into my cello and coat it with snot."

"I swear my fingers are paralysed. I won't be able to hold the bow straight."

"I think the weather is very dry. My cello's going to snap open in the middle of the ballet."

At the end of the day she squeezed me in her arms as if she was a young soldier departing to the blood-splattered trenches of a remote war.

"You'll send me positive waves of energy, won't you, Sess?"

"I'll send you a tsunami of positive energy. You'll be all right."

"I've broken the nail of my most important finger . . ."

"See you at seven, Gemz. See you at ten, Toby."

"The food will be awesome," Toby promised. "I saw Dad rolling little jam rolls from the tip of his fingers to the crease of his elbow!"

"So it's all settled?" asked Mum. "Gemma's mum is walking you back home after the party?"

"Yes, Mummy. She'll walk me back home, tuck me into bed and sing Twinkle Twinkle Little Star to me."

"Speaking of tucking, your shirt is untucked. Tuck it in."

"I'm sure that's not necessary."

"Tuck it in or you're not going."

I tucked it in.

"Right. You know that your dad and I are going to a dinner party tonight."

"Yes, Mum. I'll be fine."

"My grown-up little girl! Going to a ballet and a party on her own!"

On my own with Gemma's whole family and Toby's dad.

Gemma's parents drove me to the Concert Hall, where Gemma was doing yoga exercises to chill out before the show.

"Headstands are the best!" she said upside-down.

I sat down next to her parents and her little twin brothers, who started to voice their disgust for ballet in very realistic retching noises. Two rows down from us, Professor Philips the Elder and Professor Philips the Younger were sitting next to Mr. Franklin. I thought that this was an ideal opportunity for the police to skewer them all on a giant pole and grill them alive on the prison barbecue, but unfortunately nothing of the sort happened.

The show started and I quickly went into power-saving mode, daydreaming that I found a dinosaur egg in the Master's Garden and that my parents allowed me to keep it. This entertaining story made the ballet go much faster than I expected, and when the curtain fell I felt slightly frustrated to be interrupted in the middle of giving Cookiesaurus his first bath.

"Gemma must be super pleased that she didn't make any mistakes," I said to Mr. and Mrs. Sarland, who looked rather green, so I concluded that perhaps she might have done.

After that we migrated to the art gallery, elbowing our way past groups of musicians and dancers saying bravo to each other. Toby's dad was at the back with Toby, dishing out food and drinks. I decided to avoid the jam rolls, grabbed a strawberry, and bumped into Edwin who was carrying a huge batch of feathery wings. He disappeared with it upstairs.

"How was the show?" asked Toby.

"No idea, I was daydreaming," I replied. "You should have come! It's a great place for daydreaming, apart from the grating rattle from the orchestra pit."

A musician passing by fired a look of profound disgust at me, but it could have been because of the half-eaten armpit-flavoured jam roll she was grazing on. Then we all had to be quiet as Edwin, who had reappeared, was making a speech.

"And above all I am very grateful to Mr. Rudolph Franklin, my father, for sponsoring the show's costumes. Without Cooperture Ltd, our swans would have looked much less swan-like. Please give him a big round of applause."

The Philips brothers clapped more loudly than the rest of the group put together, and I decided I'd seen enough of this rigmarole and vaguely needed the loo, which, the wall obligingly told me, was upstairs.

At the top of the creaky staircase, I found myself in front of three doors.

The first one had an "L" on it. The second one had a "G" on it. The third one had nothing on it. I became supremely confused. Did L and G mean "Ladies" and "Gentlemen," or "Lads" and "Girls"? Why can't people express themselves more clearly? I didn't want to push the wrong door and end up in the boys' toilet. Toby tells me it is so utterly different from the girls' toilet that I would be traumatized for life.

I assumed the third door was the toilet for people who aren't too sure whether they qualify as L or G, and pushed that one.

It wasn't a toilet. It was a dark, long room, with sculptures and paintings wrapped up in bags and bubble-wrap. In a corner was the batch of wings I'd seen Edwin carry upstairs. A wide window opened on to the street, overlooking the external wall of Sidney Sussex College. I rested my elbows on the window sill, and looked up.

"Ah!" I sighed to the open skies, "To think that the world shall never know the true nature of the Professor brothers of evil and Cooperture! To think that they will roam free amongst the innocent!"

Suddenly, the door opened, and I had only a moment to dive behind a large painting of a cow in a field before someone flicked the switch on, showering the room in dull yellow light.

"Enjoying your evening, Eddie?"

"I'll enjoy it more on Sunday, when it's all done, but it's been a good night. Did you like the show, Dad?"

"Loved it. Loved it."

Someone opened the window, and the noise of a match cracking preceded the smell of cigarette smoke. Another voice joined in:

"May I? I left mine at home."

"Please, Archie, feel free. Ian?"

"I don't, thank you, Rudolph."

And just then I had a sudden bout of inspiration. Extracting my phone from my pocket, trying to make as little noise as possible, I flicked through the ridiculously small number of functions.

Call.

Text.

Phone Book.

Tooth-brushing Timer.

Alphabet Game.

Audio Message.

I selected "Audio Message" and clicked "Record."

"That's what I call a success," said Ian Philips.

"All thanks to Archie's wonderful software," replied Mr. Franklin. "Do you know, it's even more powerful than we thought—we seem to be getting very detailed information on all aspects of the users' lives which can't come only from searches. It sifts through emails too, is that correct?"

"Absolutely," Archie said. "If the word 'horse'

appears several times in someone's emails, or in their searches, they're filed as riders."

"Are your clients happy, Dad?"

"Yes, we've already had a rise in Cambridge sales. Of course, they don't know how we manage to target customers so efficiently. And once we widen it to other universities . . . and perhaps other institutions . . ."

"Aren't you glad I introduced you to Ian, Dad?" said Edwin laughingly. "He's been fantastic at putting you in touch with the right people!"

"It's easy, when you've been in the place for a long time," replied Ian Philips. "I'm a trusted member of the university. All I had to do was convince them that it's perfectly innocent."

"Which you managed superbly, I must say," remarked Mr. Franklin. "Edwin, Ian told me there had been an issue with a student guessing what was happening?"

"It's all under control, Dad. It's Stacy, the lead in the ballet—she ran into Archie's program in the computer science department when he was still working on it and she told that other girl – Jenna Jenkins—what she'd found."

"Ah! That's where it all came from."

"Archie was testing the software on the Trinity College network last Sunday, and he intercepted a conversation between Stacy and Reverend Tan—the college Chaplain. Thankfully, Archie managed to cut the connection before she told him anything of importance. I broke into his room and stole his computer a while later, just in case he'd recorded the conversation. And yesterday I went to Norwich to throw it in a rubbish tip. No one will ever find it."

"Very good. Very good. That Stacy, she's not going to tell anyone?"

"No. I negotiated with her. I'm putting her in touch with National Ballet people, kick-starting her career."

"And Jenna Jenkins?"

"We're safe there too," said Ian Philips soothingly. "There's nothing money can't buy. Actually, only yesterday I was contacted by another student who knew everything—no idea how. As easily convinced as the Jenkins girl. We've got it all under control."

"Well then—to our success!"

"To our success!"

Glasses clinking.

And suddenly another, more unexpected, noise.

You have reached the limit for audio recording. You have reached the limit for audio recording. You have reached the limit for audio recording.

Followed by the ridiculous tooth-brushing tune.

"What's this?"

"It's the cow!"

"What cow?"

"That painting!"

I saw many pairs of hands lift up the frame. And there was light.

"Sesame Seade!"

"Sesame Seade!"

"Sesame Seade!"

"Sesame Seade!"

"Wow," I said, "you all know me!"

"What are you doing here?"

"Resting behind a painting. It's all the rage."

Professor Ian Philips grabbed my shoulders and made me stand up surprisingly powerfully. "What was that about? The recording thing?"

"Oh, that! Oh, nothing!"

But they'd all turned quite pale, looking at my Phone4Kidz as if it had been a weapon of mass destruction.

"Sesame," said Edwin in a slow, high-pitched voice, "give me the phone, please."

"I can't. My parents bought it for me only yesterday. As much as I would love an excuse to give it away, they would squeeze me like a lemon until only my dry skin's left."

"Don't worry, I'll tell your parents not to punish you," purred Ian Philips in his mellifluous voice. "I know them well. They're good friends of mine."

"They wouldn't listen to you. They don't even listen to the European Union."

"Right. Let's stop playing, now," stated Mr. Franklin, and he grasped my arm. "You're going to be a good girl and give us this phone."

"Don't want!"

"Grab her!"

They each got hold of one of my limbs, which made me feel like a medieval criminal being quartered by four furious horses. Mr. Franklin covered my mouth with his hand and I struggled feverishly, kicking a vast quantity of legs, arms and faces—until I managed to wriggle free of Edwin, who was holding my right arm. Swiftly I slipped the phone into the collar of my shirt. Since—thanks to my mum—my shirt was admirably tucked in, the phone slid down and stayed stuck between my belly and my skirt in a warm little hammock.

"Abracadabra! It's vanished into thin air," I announced.

"Thin air my foot!" roared Mr. Franklin. "Turn her upside-down!"

They tried, but they hadn't thought it

through properly—instead of letting go one after the other they all dropped me at the same time, and I managed to slither out of their reach in the manner of the slimy eel. I then adopted the ways of the Australian kangaroo by hopping to the corner of the room, picking up one of the feathery wings on the way, to use as a shield.

"Now, Sesame, be reasonable," said Ian Philips in his soft voice. "The information you've got isn't valuable. No one's remotely interested in hearing it, you know. It'd be much better if you recorded yourself singing a nice little song."

"No chance! I know everything," I said. "I talked to Jenna Jenkins and to Stacy Vance. I'm the one who told Jeremy Hopkins what's going on. My friends Toby and Gemma know everything too. And no need to try and buy my silence. I don't want your money. I already get five pounds a week from my parents."

If I'd been a dog, no doubt I could have smelt their panic from my little corner. But I wasn't particularly relaxed myself, if you really need to know. There were four of them, and I was on my own, with only a shield of fluffy feathers to protect myself when I wouldn't have minded more aggressive weaponry.

"Catch her," Mr. Franklin croaked. "I don't care how."

They leapt at me—but not swiftly enough.

The best strategy, as a lioness would tell you, would have been to close up on me from all corners of the room. Instead, the fearsome foursome clownishly ran after me together, bumping into each other and stumbling over the furniture, arms outstretched and grunting like brain-craving zombies.

Ninja-like, I slipped under a table, jumped over a statue, did a cartwheel on an old armchair, swung from the ceiling lamp, and—

—found myself face to face with Edwin, right in front of the door.

How did he get there?

I ducked to the side just in time—his arms grasped cold air—and I threw myself to the ground under Mr. Franklin's legs. One karate kick to the left made a huge canvas collapse on to the professor brothers of evil. But Edwin had materialized out of nowhere again! He had the look of someone who wanted to rugby-tackle me.

Not fast enough!

I sprang up into the ether, and one second later, I landed next to the window.

The window was open. And on the window sill was a squirrel, who leapt swiftly away.

And suddenly something happened in my brain.

You know what I told you about the number of connections in your brain being equal to the number of stars in the universe? That's how it works.

You see a squirrel.

This reminds you of Mrs. Appleyard's video of gliding squirrels.

Then you notice that you're holding feathery wings.

And then you remember Edwin saying that

they're solid little things that could hold your weight.

Your brain puts two and two together, and says, "Glide."

I put on the wings, grabbed the straps, climbed on the window sill, and—

"No! Catch her!"

The wind slapped me as I jumped, and the gale met the wings. Immediately I slowed down, as if I was sliding on invisible rails of air—crossing the street, soaring above the walls of Sidney Sussex College.

Going down a bit quicker there, with less wind to hold me up . . .

"Oh, look!" said someone below me. "A swan!"

Down, down, down, down.

"Oh my God!" someone else exclaimed. "It's not a swan! It's—"

And as I crashed not very elegantly on to the soft grass of Sidney Sussex, I heard, in perfect unison, two voices which I really could have done without:

"SOPHIE MARGARET CATRIONA SEADE!"

XI

The rest is history. You probably don't want to hear about my getting the Keys to the City from the hands of the Duke and Duchess of Cambridge. Well, at least I hope you don't want to hear about it, because it didn't happen, much to my and Toby's and Gemma's indignation.

What happened was this: my parents, in fits, dropped their plates and glasses to pick me up from the ground. Apparently the Master of Sidney Sussex had invited them to a quiet little shebang in the college gardens. I'd sort of ruined their evening, but that's normal. I was rushed to A&E, even though I was fine, just a few ruffled feathers and a bruise on my knee which I swear had been there before. The Fellows who were dining in the Sidney Sussex gardens, including the Vice-Chancellor, followed us to hospital in their gowns and waited outside like a troop of worried-looking ravens until I came out triumphantly.

"Victory!" I told my fan club. "Not the merest plaster anywhere on my body! Sesame Seade is not a swan, but she's as solid as a stone!"

Then I was taken to the police station, where I produced my phone, upon which no one could refrain from laughing. I played the recording. They heard it all. They noted it all down. They told my meek-looking Mum and Dad they should have listened to me.

"I'm always telling them that, but they never listen. Do you, Mum?"

"Do I what, darling?"

It's a hopeless business.

"Can I go in your car for the car chase?" I asked.

"What car chase?" chuckled the Inspector.

"The one you're about to have to catch the Franklins and the Philipses."

"Don't think there's going to be a car chase, love," said the Inspector, which saddened me no end.

There was no car chase. Edwin Franklin and his father, who had stayed, rather stupidly, at the art gallery, were caught there and not even handcuffed. The Philips brothers were found at the Fitzwilliam museum destroying their computers, but not quickly enough for all the information to disappear. Jenna Jenkins was woken up by a phone call from the Inspector. Stacy Vance was dragged to the police station to be interrogated.

As for Jeremy, well, I mysteriously forgot to mention him to the Inspector. I was about to, but got distracted by a crack on the wall that looked a bit like a kite-surfing hippopotamus. After all, he hadn't technically taken any money, and *UniGossip* still needed him. And maybe I did too.

And that was all.

I thought I would testify in court, make a tear-jerking speech, explain every little detail of my adventure! I thought Toby and Gemma would be called as witnesses! I thought I would be allowed to publicly whip Edwin, Mr. Franklin and the Philips brothers! I thought I would shake the Queen's hand and be thanked on behalf of the whole country!

But no.

"Are you ready for school?"

"Mother! I cannot go to school today!"

"And why not, pray?"

"Because I've had a close brush with death and bandits! I've saved everyone's Internet privacy! I've made one of the country's biggest companies collapse!"

But I was pushed into the Smurfmobile like any other schoolgirl! Me, Sesame Seade, Cambridge's number one supersleuth! But then I remembered that school meant I could tell everyone my story, and I calmed down.

"Are you super furious, Mummy?"

"Why would I be?"

"Because College has lost all the Cooperture money."

"Well," Mum laughed, "I'm sure we'll get much more in compensation when the trial takes place."

More money. More money. Even more money.

"Can I have a pocket money rise?"

"No."

"Ten little pounds a week!"

"No."

"Nine, then."

"No."

"Seven? Six and a half?"

"Six and a half, at your next birthday."

"But that's in six months!"

"It'll give you time to get used to the idea of having such a fortune at your disposal."

Later when I came back home I found an electric guitar on my bed.

My parents are sometimes cool.

And you know what, it doesn't matter that I
didn't get the Order of the British Empire or
the Nobel Prize for Peace. Supersleuths don't
need that. All they need is the satisfaction of
having done a good job, which I had, with the
added thrill of having used strange ways of
going from one place to another, which I had. It
was a bit awkward because suddenly everyone
at school wanted their pictures taken with me
on their very cool phones, but you get used to
the popularity. And then it all died out anyway
when Suzanne Windermere got her new sparkly
pink braces.

"Sophie, you have a visitor," said Dad, making it
sound like an ogre was trying to force his way
into my room.

"Oh, hi, Jeremy!"

"Hi, Sesame. May I come in?"

"Sure, if you don't smash up the place like

212

you did in your own room."

He sat on the end of my bed. "Yeah, about the Cooperture thing, I just wanted to say . . ."

"That you're very sorry, and that money made you mad. I know."

"No, that's not what I wanted to say."

"Really? What did you want to say?"

"I wanted to say that you're a mentalist, you absolute idiot—throwing yourself out of a window like that! Promise me you'll never do it again!"

"All right. You can always buy me a helicopter with your next bribe."

He went raspberry red. "OK, thanks for not telling anyone, Sesame. I, er, I really appreciate it. It wasn't like me to say yes to those guys. So, thank you, and, well, I guess—I'm sorry, and all that."

I replied, "You are forgiven, my child, as my dad says to everyone. Though he didn't say it to me when I skated into that ugly jade lion in the living-room."

"Right. I have another thing to ask you. The

University's letting Jenna come back despite the whole affair, but she's not going to work for *UniGossip* any more. I'm the new Editor-in-Chief. And I'd like you to be in our team of investigators. Now that we know you're both a super sleuth and an incorruptible one."

He whispered that, of course, because Mum and Dad downstairs would probably not approve.

"Oh, Jeremy, that would be the most beauteous thing ever! I can't wait! Wow, I have a job—that's just—it's just—"

"All right, don't be too loud. You won't be credited in the mag, of course, but if I call you and ask you to go spy on someone . . ."

"Who're you gonna call? Sesame Seade!'" I sang.

"Doesn't fit. Anyway. I'll try not to send you on missions that are too dangerous. . . ."

"I can deal with danger!"

"It'll also mean not being seen, and not boasting when you do manage to find something."

"Say no more! As long as I can help the community, I will. It is my mission. My burden. My responsibility."

We shook hands and shared a Battenberg cake to seal our professional relationship. Peter Mortimer nicked Jeremy's slice before he could eat it, which annoyed Jeremy a little, but he should have known better and wolfed it all down before the feline could.

"Right," I said. "When do I start?"

"Well," Jeremy replied, "as it happens, I just got a phone call this morning, and apparently, strange noises have been heard in the cellars of Clare College. . . ."

Acknowledgments

I've never written an acknowledgments page before, but so many people have indirectly contributed to Sesame that this time I can't keep up the pretense that I've done it all on my own.

Christ's College has been my home for the past seven years. Much like Sesame, I've grown up there. A very special thank-you to Don and Tod, the Porters, who did much more than lend their names, and to the Master, Professor Frank Kelly, who thinks Sesame should focus a little bit more on her science homework!

Thank you so, so much to my very precious book-lover friends, Anna, Lauren and Erin, who've been adorable to me over the past two years of doubts, joys and worries since I started to write in English. My mum's also been doing that for the past twenty years since I started to write in French. Merci Maman.

Professors Maria Nikolajeva and Morag Styles have been the fairy godmothers of my graduate life. They taught me everything I know about children's literature and never worried that I was writing books alongside my PhD thesis.

Kirsty McLachlan is the loveliest agent imaginable, and the calmest in two times of crisis: no publishers, and then too many. Her advice and suggestions are always spot-on. As for my editor, Ellen Holgate, I couldn't have asked for a more enthusiastic, creative and witty friend to work with.

Finally, Simon, I wrote most of this book to the tune of your virtuosic piano-playing. You were one of the first to read it. I will always have so much tenderness for our years together.